Kate's eyes were hostile and cold

Her gaze swept past Courtney and rested on the white folds of her discarded wedding dress.

"Very virginal," Kate said lightly. "But are you sure that's what Blair wants?"

Courtney stared back at her steadily. "Another warning, Kate?" she asked coolly, but her heart thudded as she wondered exactly how much of her new husband's confidence Kate enjoyed. It made her skin crawl to think the other woman might know about the desperate bargain she had tried to make with Blair. Perhaps Kate and he had laughed about it together.

"I wouldn't want you to have unrealistic ideas about your marriage," Kate said venomously. "You're being married for expediency—for no other reason. You always were a child, Courtney, and Blair needs a woman. Never forget that."

SARA CRAVEN
is also the author of these

Harlequin Presents

and this
Harlequin Romance

Many of these books are available at your local bookseller.

For a free catalog listing all titles currently available,
send your name and address to:

HARLEQUIN READER SERVICE
1440 South Priest Drive, Tempe, AZ 85281
Canadian address: Stratford, Ontario N5A 6W2

SARA CRAVEN

sup with the devil

Harlequin Books

TORONTO • NEW YORK • LOS ANGELES • LONDON
AMSTERDAM • PARIS • SYDNEY • HAMBURG
STOCKHOLM • ATHENS • TOKYO • MILAN

Harlequin Presents first edition June 1983
ISBN 0-373-10599-1

Original hardcover edition published in 1983
by Mills & Boon Limited

CHAPTER ONE

'So when do the bulldozers move in?'

Robin Lincoln flushed angrily. 'Oh, for heaven's sake, Courtney! It won't be that bad.'

'No?' his sister queried ironically. 'Judging by these——' she swept a contemptuous hand over the pile of plans and folders lying between them on the living room table '—it's about as bad as it could be. You surely can't imagine the local people are going to stand for anything like this? Why, they'll be up in arms as soon as the news gets out!'

'Well, I don't happen to share your opinion,' Robin said defensively. 'I admit it may take them a while to accustom themselves, but . . .'

'A while?' Courtney's echo was derisive. 'When they hear that Hunters Court—the house that's been looked on as the manor all these years—has been bought up by a consortium who want to turn it into a cheap country club?'

Her brother glared at her. 'There you go again—sitting in judgment. Just because it's poor old Monty!'

'Hardly an apt description—or one that he would appreciate.' Courtney raised her eyebrows. 'Wealthy middle-aged Monty would be more to the point.'

Robin's mouth turned down sullenly. 'You really dislike him, don't you?'

'I've hardly made any secret of it,' Courtney returned crisply. 'I think he's a repulsive little creep, and that this—scheme he's dreamed up is typical of him. The only thing I can't understand is how you ever got involved with him in the first place.'

'Oh no, you wouldn't understand,' Robin said savagely. 'You don't like success, do you, Courtney? You're frightened of it. Ever since we lost Hunters Court and Father had that second stroke you decided it

5

was safer to settle for this—rabbit hutch, and a dull future just ahead of the breadline, rather than make any attempt to recoup what we lost, but I'm not prepared to do that, and you don't like it.'

Courtney sat down wearily on one of the elderly chairs which flanked the table. 'Rob, that's not true! Do you think I haven't dreamed as you have of getting Hunters Court back somehow? But I've always known it wasn't possible. Even before that—other business, Father was having a job to keep it going. You know that. Houses like Hunters Court eat money, and their appetite gets bigger every year.'

'Of course I know it,' Robin said shortly. 'Why do you think I agreed to act for the consortium? Because it's a way—probably the only way that we'll ever get Hunters Court back.'

'But we won't be getting it back,' Courtney argued. 'It will belong to them. All you'll be is the manager—a paid employee. It won't be the same. It can't.'

Rob shrugged. 'Then it will have to do,' he said. 'I'm not dogsbodying at Carteret's for the rest of my life. I'm sick of being treated as a charity case. Sick of the whispered remarks. "Lincoln? Lincoln? Any relation to the man whose partner embezzled all that money?" '

Courtney sighed inwardly. Three years ago Geoffrey Devereux had been arrested at Heathrow, after a spot audit had revealed discrepancies in the handling of clients' money. He had been charged with embezzlement, and bail had been opposed while further enquiries were made, but he had died of a heart attack while on remand, leaving James Lincoln, the head of the firm, facing ruin, and the knowledge that his friend and partner of many years' standing had betrayed him.

When the full amount of the liability that Devereux had created became known, James Lincoln himself had become ill, suffering two strokes, the second of which had left him semi-paralysed and hardly able to speak.

Within a matter of weeks Courtney and Robin found their world had turned upside down. Geoffrey Devereux had died without making any kind of confession, or even a hint as to what he'd done with the thousands of pounds he had stolen. But it had to be repaid somehow, and Hunters Court, which had been the Lincoln family home for generations, was put on the market.

Robin's dream of becoming a racing driver died there and then, under the necessity of earning some kind of living, and he reluctantly accepted his godfather's offer of employment in his merchant bank.

Courtney, in the middle of an A-level course at her expensive boarding school, abandoned her plans for university, and thanked heaven for the shorthand and typing option she had taken instead of the needlework she loathed. She had to leave school because there was no more money forthcoming for fees.

The cottage, offered to them by the owner of the neighbouring estate, Colonel FitzHugh, was a godsend, even if it did seem like the rabbit hutch of Robin's description after the spaciousness of Hunters Court. And because the Colonel was an old friend of their father's, they only paid a minimum rental for it.

She said gently, 'Rob, mud sticks, that's inevitable, but it will pass. The job at Carteret's may not be very exciting, but it's security. Don't throw it away for some chancy scheme put forward by a man you hardly know.'

Robin looked mutinous. 'We knew Geoffrey Devereux, or thought we did, and a lot of good it did us. All you have against Monty is sheer female prejudice.'

There was a certain amount of justice in that, Courtney was forced to concede. She knew no actual harm of Montague Pallister and the companies with which he was associated, but instinct told her that he was a speculator, whose genial manner concealed a ruthless determination to squeeze the last penny out of any project with which he was connected, and the thought of such a man getting his hands on Hunters Court frankly nauseated her.

It had hurt when the Hallorans had bought the

estate, but they were nice people and had looked after it well. Courtney was disappointed that they too were being forced to sell, but she understood that Mrs Halloran's health demanded a warmer winter climate than Britain had to offer. She had hoped that some like-minded people would come along and buy Hunters Court, but the economic recession had made many potential buyers rethink the wisdom of acquiring a country estate, however modest, and Courtney had come reluctantly to realise that when Hunters Court was put up for auction, it would probably be bought by some commercial concern—as a small private hotel, perhaps, or a nursing home.

She had not then associated Montague Pallister's arrival on the scene with the sale of Hunters Court, and looking back, she supposed she had been naïve.

At first she had accepted Robin's airy explanation that he had met Monty through the bank, and that he had given him some advice over investments. Robin certainly seemed to have more money at his disposal these days, and Courtney wished she could have felt more gratefully disposed towards Monty Pallister, but it was impossible. He was too well-dressed, too opulent, and the way she had seen him looking at herself when he thought he was unobserved made her feel ill.

Because he was ostensibly a friend of Robin's, he often visited the cottage, although it was too small for him to actually stay there, to Courtney's relief. Instead he stayed at the local inn, which had a good reputation for its food and accommodation, and when he was at the cottage Courtney could usually find an excuse to be elsewhere. After his visits, she always imagined that there were traces of him round the place, as if he left a trail like a slug.

But there had been no clues that he wanted Hunters Court, she thought bitterly. That had been a well-kept secret, even though he must have had architects and surveyors working on the project even before the estate had been put on the market if the volume of material they had produced was anything to go by. She had sat up the greater part of the previous night reading it, trying and failing to come to terms with what was planned. The house itself would survive, in spite of internal alterations to extend the dining room, and provide at least two bars. But the stables and outbuildings would vanish, to be rebuilt as mews-style cottages to be offered for sale on a time-share basis. The sunken garden would disappear too, and be replaced by a swimming pool. The small park would be transformed into a nine-hole golf course, and the walled rose garden would turn into tennis courts.

On paper, it did not sound so bad, but Courtney had seen glossy brochures advertising other projects in which Monty Pallister had been involved. A quick financial return rather than quality seemed to be the underlying principle, and Courtney could not bear to think of the house which had been her home for seventeen years being sacrificed to that. It was a foolish thought—as if stones and mortar could bleed—but last night as she'd read the reports and looked at the plans and sketches, she hadn't felt foolish at all, just blazingly angry.

This morning, she'd tried to explain to Robin how she felt, but she'd known from the start that it was useless. He didn't want to understand.

All he knew was that at tomorrow's auction he would be bidding for Hunters Court on behalf of the consortium, and just for a while he could pretend that he was buying it back for himself, his birthright. The reality, Courtney thought, would be very different, but then a sense of reality was not Robin's strong point, and never had been.

He'd complained that his job at Carteret's was a dead end, but Courtney felt that if he'd settled down to it, Philip Carteret would have seen that he was properly rewarded. As it was, over the past weeks Robin had hardly been there, and she had no idea what excuses he made for his absences, if he even bothered.

Now, she said quietly, 'Rob, why did you never tell me what was going on?'

He shrugged. 'I was going to tell you today, as a matter of fact, only old FitzHugh beat me to it. How the hell did he find out, I'd like to know?'

She shook her head. 'This is a small place. A rumour doesn't take long to get round. And he's a friend of Frank Mottram the auctioneer. He probably mentioned that you were interested. Anyway, what does it matter? They don't know the truth.'

She'd been on her way home from the office early yesterday because the man she worked for was going away to a conference, and had offered her a few days off while he was away to compensate for a lot of extra work she'd done recently. She had agreed with pleasure. She wanted to decorate her bedroom, and she'd bought the paper and paint several weeks before. She had stopped at the village store to buy some bread, and Colonel FitzHugh had just been coming out. He had paused smilingly.

'Well, my dear, this is great news! The Lincolns belong at Hunters Court, and I wish Rob every success at the auction. I don't imagine he'll have much competition—certainly not from local people anyway.'

Courtney had said something in reply, and driven straight home, the bread forgotten. Just for a while, she had enjoyed her fantasies too. Rob was going to buy Hunters Court. They would be home again. Father could leave the nursing home at last, and come to live with them again. But the euphoria was only momentary. Then the questions began. Where was Rob getting the money? She knew that, through Monty Pallister, he had been dabbling in the Stock Market, but surely he hadn't made enough through his transactions to meet even the quite modest reserve the Hallorans had placed on Hunters Court. Or had Uncle Philip by some miracle offered to lend him the money? It didn't seem likely. Philip Carteret was a shrewd financier, who had once described Hunters Court and houses like it as 'albatrosses'. He and James Lincoln had almost quarrelled over it.

She had intended to phone Rob at Carteret's, but she

didn't have to, because he was there at home. He'd been telephoning, as it happened. He was just replacing the receiver as she walked in, and looking incredibly pleased with himself.

Courtney had stood for a long moment looking at him. She felt frightened suddenly, although she didn't know why.

She said, 'Colonel FitzHugh tells me you're going to bid for Hunters Court at the auction on Friday. It can't be true. We—we can't afford it. You know that.'

Rob said, 'We don't have to.' There was a kind of triumph in his voice. 'Sister dear, we're going to have all the comforts of home—and none of the expense. It's all fixed.'

He had told her the whole story there and then, going out to the car and bringing in the briefcase full of files and plans that she had never seen before.

She had listened to him numbly, wondering how he could bear to refer to Hunters Court in such terms, her emotions in shock, rejecting every persuasive phrase as it fell from his lips.

'A country club—leisure facilities—sauna and gym— a first class restaurant.' His voice had risen with excitement, his hands gesticulating as he sketched out the fate Monty Pallister had designed for Hunters Court.

Her immediate reaction had been, 'It will never work. Local people don't go in for that sort of thing.'

He looked impatient. 'It won't just be for locals. Haven't you been listening? The people who buy the cottages will use it mainly, although it will be open to outsiders. Monty opened a similar place in the south-west two years ago. It's been incredibly successful, and this will be too. He has all the right contacts.'

Courtney's mouth moved stiffly. 'And he has you.'

'What's that supposed to mean?' He had glared at her.

'So this is what he wanted. You—to act as front man for him. I suppose he thought if the word got out that he wanted the estate, the price would go sky-high.'

'Well, naturally. And he has business rivals. He doesn't want any of them getting ahead of him.'

'Oh, naturally,' Courtney said bitterly.

They had argued all evening, and she'd sat up for most of the night going through the file over and over again, trying to derive some crumb of comfort, but in vain.

And it looked no better in the pallid sunlight of a February morning.

She said, 'What are you going to tell Daddy?'

'I've already told him.' Another flash of triumph.

She looked at him helplessly. 'And how did he react.'

Robin shrugged. 'Generally in favour. He knows what it will mean for all of us. And he'll get out of that damned nursing home. On the salary I'll be getting for managing the country club, I can afford a live-in nurse for him.'

Courtney said drily, 'It all sounds too good to be true.' And it did. What did Rob know about managing anything that could justify the kind of salary he was talking about? 'And when you say "all of us", please don't include me. I don't want any part of this, or anything else that Monty Pallister has dreamed up.'

He gave her an impatient look. 'Don't be a fool! Of course you're included. There'll be plenty of secretarial work once it gets started—reception too, if you fancy it.'

'The hostess with the mostest,' Courtney said ironically. 'But I don't fancy it, Rob. I don't want any of it. I like my job, and I'll stick to that, thanks.'

He stared at her. 'You can't be serious!'

'What makes you think that?' She gave him a straight glance. 'I'd have been against this scheme if a complete stranger had been involved, and the fact that it's you makes no difference at all. When the news gets out locally, everyone will be against you. Don't you realise that?'

He said savagely, 'If you think I'm going to stay a loser all my life just to please the neighbours, then you can think again. Where were they when we needed them?'

'That's not fair,' said Courtney in a low voice. 'We've received a lot of kindness—this cottage, for example. And although he's not a neighbour, Uncle Philip . . .'

'Uncle Philip!' Robin was derisive. 'You sound like a child! I suppose if Geoffrey Devereux were to walk in through that door now, you'd call him "Uncle" too.'

Courtney sighed. 'I probably would at that. I can't just shake off the habit of a lifetime. And he always was like an uncle to us, after all.'

There was a trace of malice in Robin's smile. 'And his nephew who was such a constant visitor in the old days. How would you greet him? As Cousin Blair?'

For a long bleak moment a disturbing image rose in Courtney's mind—a lean, tanned face cast in bitter lines, hard hazel eyes, glittering with anger and contempt, and on one high cheekbone, a trickle of blood. Just for that moment it was as if Robin's words had evoked him, and he was there in the room, a physical presence rather than a figment of her imagination. And just for that moment she was back in the study at Hunters Court, her father slumped grey-faced in the chair beside her, while she screamed, 'Get out of here! Get out! Leave us alone. Haven't you done enough harm? Can't you see he's ill?'

And his voice—not the faintly amused drawl she had always hated, but harsh and raw. 'He deserves to be ill—and more.'

It had sounded like a curse, as if he was predicting some future vengeance, and it had frightened her. And when James Lincoln had collapsed with his first stroke not long afterwards, she had always remembered.

She controlled a shiver. Why had Robin had to remind her of him now? It was a long time since she'd allowed herself to think of Blair Devereux.

Aloud she said coolly, 'I think not. I was never prepared to go to those lengths, even in the old days. I dislike Blair Devereux more than I do your friend Mr Pallister, and that's saying something.'

It had always been there, she thought, ever since Blair

had come into their lives. Not so much dislike at first as
a bewildered resentment. Geoffrey Devereux had been a
childless widower, and over the years he had become a
close part of the family. He came and went at Hunters
Court as if it was his own home, and Courtney in
particular saw him as a surrogate uncle.

Blair's arrival on the scene had been a shock and a
disappointment. She'd been used to thinking of Uncle
Geoffrey as being alone in the world, and now it
seemed he had a nephew with a prior claim on his time
and attention, because Blair's parents were dead.

If he'd been a child like herself, she could have
understood, perhaps, but he was already a man, ten
years older than herself, seven years older than Robin.
An attractive man, she had come unwillingly to realise
as time passed, tall and slim with thick tawny hair
which curled slightly, and hazel eyes mocking under
heavy lids.

When Blair was at Hunters Court, together with her
father and Geoffrey Devereux, he seemed to complete a
charmed circle from which she and Robin were
excluded as children. Courtney didn't want to feel
excluded. Because she and her brother were at boarding
school, their time at Hunters Court was limited, and
Blair's visits during the holidays always seemed to cast
a shadow over her happiness.

Nothing seemed to work—either behaving out-
rageously in order to attract attention, or pretending
that he didn't exist. Whatever she tried made little
difference. The most reaction she ever got from him was
a bored, 'Don't be more of a brat than you can help,
Courtney.'

She simmered with loathing of him, and it wasn't
helped by Robin undergoing a type of adolescent hero-
worship for him, making her feel more isolated than
ever.

That passed, of course, and as she herself moved
through her own adolescence towards womanhood,
she found reluctantly that her feelings towards Blair
were becoming more ambivalent. But his abrupt

arrivals were always a shock, setting her at odds with herself, overturning her fragile girl's poise. She had come to think of him as a kind of bird of ill omen, hovering and dangerous on the corner of her life, and later, as that life had crashed in ruins about her, she had realised how accurate that perception of him had been.

But he had been the sole shadow in the last golden summer before everything had slid so suddenly and frighteningly away. She'd been having such a wonderful time. She'd been reckless with invitations to stay and Hunters Court had been filled with her school friends. Patterson who looked after the grounds had fixed up a badminton net on the lawn at the side of the house, and they'd played desultory matches in the heat, then lounged with cold drinks beside the small lake, talking about everything and anything—their forthcoming examinations, their dreams and aspirations.

Then Blair had arrived, and all that closeness and empathy had been shattered. She saw it happen, saw the other girls looking at him, sidelong glances at first and then quite openly. Saw the focus of attention slip away making them all not so much friends as rivals. Saw him spoil everything.

Once again she felt that she was the outsider, and she hated him for it. It made no difference that he never actively encouraged any of them. He was civil, but aloof, and not even the most blatantly flirtatious advances did anything to penetrate the wall of reserve he seemed to have built round himself. One by one they all tried to get through to him and failed, and were resigned or sulky or despondent according to temperament.

Courtney didn't know which side she despised the most, or even why. She sat miserably listening to the electric silence which descended whenever Blair appeared, watching them watching him, and realising that charmed circle of girlhood had gone for ever.

Then she found they were watching her and speculating, and that was the worst of all.

'You never mentioned him,' Anna Harper said one afternoon, when they were all by the lake. 'Not once.'

Courtney shrugged, feeling awkward. 'It never occurred to me.' She tried to explain several times that to her he was simply Blair, Uncle Geoffrey's nephew, and a thorn in her flesh, but she knew they hadn't believed her.

'He behaves as if we're invisible!' someone else wailed.

Kate Lydyard, who was trailing her fingers in the water, smiled, her eyes going slyly to Courtney. Kate was the oldest in the group, already eighteen, with an extra confidence and self-assurance. Courtney had always admired her, and her cool blonde good looks, but since Kate had been at Hunters Court, she had discovered she didn't really like her very much.

Now Kate moved her hand sharply, sending a spray of glistening droplets into the air. She said softly, 'That's because he's waiting for Courtney.'

They were all looking at her, suspicious and envious at the same time.

She said sharply, 'Then he'll wait for ever.' Her voice rang clearly through the warm afternoon. She saw a movement on the terrace and shading her eyes realised that he was there. She could have screamed with vexation, but consoled herself with the reflection that he was too far away to have overheard the entire conversation, so that her final comment, if he'd picked it up, would have been meaningless. At least she hoped so.

But later when they met in the drawing room for tea, she wasn't too sure. Each time she glanced up, Blair seemed to be watching her, and while there was amusement in his eyes, there was speculation too, which she found frankly alarming. She was beginning to wonder whether her words of angry refutal to Kate hadn't lit some kind of slow fuse, and ask herself what she could do to evade the inevitable explosion.

But as time passed and nothing happened, she told herself on a rising tide of relief that she had been mistaken, that she'd read altogether too much into the situation.

Blair left the next day, and by the end of the week her party had broken up too, somewhat to her relief, she realised unhappily. The golden days had taken on an acid tinge, although some of the old camaraderie had returned following Blair's departure. Things would improve, she thought optimistically, when they all met again at school in September.

A few days later, she had been in the rose garden cutting some blooms for her father's study, when some sixth sense warned her that she was no longer alone. She looked warily over her shoulder and saw Blair standing in the arched gateway watching her. She met the cool, assessing glance he sent her with an uneasiness she was incapable of concealing.

'What a charming picture.' He walked unhurriedly towards her. 'The young English maiden among the roses.'

There was nothing she could take exception to or even deny in his actual words, but the jibing tone in which they were uttered was a different matter. She turned away deliberately, flushing with annoyance, totally on edge. He'd never sought her out like this before—so why . . .?

She went on cutting roses and putting them in her basket, almost at random, only too aware of Blair at her shoulder, wishing there was something other than the murmur of the bees to break the tension of the silence between them.

At least he said, 'How old are you, Courtney?'

She shot him a startled look. 'Seventeen.'

'Then I'm a year out,' he said. 'I'd have said sixteen.'

'In other words, I'm young for my age. Thank you so much!'

'That's not what I meant at all,' he returned. 'There's a well-known saying about being sixteen which I'd say applies to you. And before you start bristling, it has nothing to do with the age of consent,' he added, his mouth twisting in the mockery which always caught her on the raw.

'I know the saying you mean,' she said tightly. 'It's a bit old hat these days, surely. We are in the nineteen-eighties.'

'Only just. Although what difference the decade we live in is supposed to make I fail to understand. If it was the year 2001, it wouldn't make you any less nervous. And it confirms what I just said.'

'What do you mean?'

He took the basket from her slackening grip and put it down on the gravelled walk. The hazel eyes weren't laughing now. They were curiously intent, and Courtney swallowed, aware of the oddest aching sensation in the pit of her stomach.

He said quietly, 'That this has never happened to you before.'

His mouth on hers was warm and firm and incredibly sensuous. She stiffened instinctively, her hands coming up in open panic to thrust him away, but he made no attempt to draw her into a closer embrace. And before she could marshal her thoughts sufficiently to decide on some form of protest, the kiss was over.

'How dare you!' she almost choked.

He smiled down at her lazily. 'You'll find I dare quite easily. For ever is a long time, Courtney. I merely decided I'd waited long enough.'

So he had heard, and drawn totally accurate conclusions. She breathed inwardly, but refused to let him guess. She shrugged.

'I presumed you feel you've made some kind of point. Please don't expect me to be grateful.'

'No, I won't do that.' He handed back the basket, his smile widening into a grin. 'I'd prefer something warmer in the way of emotion than mere gratitude.'

'What a shame,' she said too sweetly. 'I think you must be confusing me with some of my friends.'

'Now what do I infer from that? That you're immune?'

A glint in the hazel eyes warned her in time that affirmation might be reckless. Her thoughtless words to

Kate Lydyard had already provided him with one challenge; she didn't want to compound the offence. Besides, she wasn't altogether sure any more that she could plead immunity or even indifference. She was still shaking inside, and her mouth felt soft and tremulous. She tried to explain away her acute vulnerability by telling herself she was ashamed because Blair had so easily guessed her total lack of any kind of experience, but she knew it wasn't as simple as that. She had a confused feeling that nothing might ever be simple again.

She couldn't think of a single thing to say, and when she saw him move, take a step towards her, she panicked, backing away straight into a rose bush. The thorns caught her in an instant, fastening themselves into the thin cotton blouse and the brief denim skirt.

She said, 'Oh, hell!' in a low, furious voice, and twisted trying to free herself.

'Keep still,' Blair directed. 'You'll tear your clothes, if not your skin, if you struggle like that.'

His hands were sure and expert as they released her, but she was in an agony of tension, and not because she was afraid of being scratched by the murderous thorns.

When he had finished, she said, 'Thank you,' staring down at the neatly raked gravel at her feet.

He said mockingly, 'That really caused you some grief, didn't it, Courtney?' He sighed with a trace of impatience. 'But you don't have to worry. You're not going to be rushed into anything you're not ready for—I promise you that.'

Her heart began to thud slowly and uncomfortably, as she tried to make sense of what he'd just said. Why did he talk about promises, and about not rushing her? He couldn't pretend that one sunlit kiss had made any real difference to a man of his age and experience, no matter what effect it might have had on her. A totally calculated effect, as she now realised.

She said hurriedly, 'I don't know what you're talking about. And you'll have to excuse me now, please. I have things to do.'

'Flowers to arrange, for one thing,' he said, sounding amused. He reached to one of the bushes beside him, the lean strong fingers moving among the stems. He said, 'Keep this one for yourself.'

It was the most perfect bloom, just beginning to open from its bud, creamy white with a hint of pink in the furled centre. Courtney stared down at it as if she was transfixed.

He went on, 'You don't have to invent chores and run away, Courtney. I'm going now. But I'll be back.'

And that was a promise too, she thought, as she stood in the sunlight, and held the rose he had given her.

Even though three years had passed, Courtney could still remember the welter of emotion which had assailed her. What a child she had been! How accurately Blair Devereux had assessed her.

She had kept the rose in a crystal vase on her dressing table. It had been the last thing she had seen as she closed her eyes at night, and the first thing she had looked for too. Probably Blair had known that too. That would have been his intention. A constant reminder to keep her on her toes, and make her count the passing of the summer days.

But before the rose had begun to fade, that magic golden time was over for ever. The realisation that something was terribly wrong had dawned on her slowly. She had seen her father looking pale and ill, and questioned him, but he had dismissed her queries lightly, blaming overwork and the heat. Each evening he shut himself into the study, eating his dinner from a tray, and spending most of his time on the telephone. She tried to discuss her worries with Rob, but he didn't seem interested.

The news of Geoffrey Devereux's arrest at Heathrow had been like a bombshell. Overnight, she saw her father dwindle into an elderly man, and became aware that tension hung over their lives like a clenched fist.

She couldn't believe what had happened. She kept repeating to herself, 'It isn't true. It can't be true,' like some mourning litany. It was impossible that the warm, kindly man who had been so safe and secure a part of her life for so long could be a betrayer, a criminal. If it was true, then any disaster seemed possible.

And disaster had come, each one falling like a hammerblow. She had tried hard to close her mind to that time, to look forward, only forward to a future which had to be better, but now she couldn't stop the memories crowding thick and fast.

Blair had been one of them. She had never wanted to think about him again, but Robin's casual comment had opened the floodgates.

He'd said he would be back, and he came, but not as she could ever have imagined. When he came, he was full of a dark and savage anger, which she supposed was natural because Geoffrey Devereux was his uncle, and was in prison on remand. It was a shattering shock for anyone, and they were terribly upset too, but that had not seemed to occur to him. And the first she had known of his presence in the house was when she had come downstairs that evening and heard the raised angry voices coming from the study . . .

Rob said curiously, 'What's the matter? You look like a ghost?'

She felt like a ghost, Courtney thought hysterically. There were ghosts everywhere, rising out of the past to torment her just when she thought they had been laid to rest for ever.

He said, 'You're not still brooding about Monty, are you? For heaven's sake, Courtney . . .'

'About him,' she said tightly. 'Among other things.' The cottage suddenly seemed as small as he'd claimed, the walls closing in on her, even though she wasn't normally claustrophobic. She swallowed. 'I—I'm going out for a while. I think I'll drive over to Hunters Court.'

'What on earth for?'

She shrugged. 'To see it one last time—before it comes under the hammer in more ways than one,' she added ironically.

Rob flushed. 'It won't be as bad as you think.'

She lifted her hands, then let them fall helplessly at her side. It would be every bit as bad. She'd seen glossy brochures about some of Monty Pallister's past projects—executive housing that seemed to have been specifically designed with midgets in mind, highly glazed office blocks, and gaudy shopping precincts in concrete in what Courtney suspected had once been pleasant high streets. Everything he touched, he spoiled, she thought, and Hunters Court would be no exception, and there had been a time when Rob would have seen this too. Now, he seemed to be deliberately blinding himself to the realities. She had always known how bitterly he had resented the disgrace that their association with Geoffrey Devereux had brought on them. To Rob, Monty Pallister was a way back to the good times.

But he's wrong, she thought. Monty Pallister is a user. He doesn't allow himself to be used. Rob could be heading for trouble if he thought otherwise. Then she checked herself. What use was there in worrying? He was set on this path, and nothing she had been able to say had deterred him one jot.

She started the Mini and drove with extra care out of the cramped yard, because she was on edge and that was when accidents happened.

As she drove through the lanes, she began to make herself relax. It was a pretty drive, especially today with a pale February sun straggling over the bare trees, and lifting a faint mist from the wet fields. The last week had been cold and raining, and it would have been appropriate to her mood if today had been the same. She didn't want the promise of the sun. She felt as bleak as if spring would never come.

She thought perhaps she would leave. Good secretaries were always in demand, and there was nothing to keep her in the area. She would go somewhere else, and make a new life for herself, and forget everything that had happened, and everything that was going to happen.

There was a high stone wall concealing Hunters Court from the road. Courtney wondered whether that would remain when the alterations began. After all, Monty Pallister wouldn't want to hide away his new possession. He'd want to advertise it, probably with neon lights, and she didn't want to be here to see that.

The tall iron gates at the end of the drive stood open, but the estate agents' sign had gone, she noticed. There had been high winds for a few days along with the rain, and it had blown down, and probably the agent had decided that as the auction was so near it wasn't worth putting it up again. They would wait until they could put a sign saying 'Sold' up, because that would be a much better advertisement.

She drove slowly, looking steadily ahead of her at the view she had seen so many countless times, etching it on to her brain for all eternity.

By some irony, the house had never looked lovelier, its mellow stones unmasked by creeper. The Hallorans had cherished it, and it sprawled contentedly in the sunlight.

She blinked suddenly, because just for a moment the years rolled away, and she was a much younger Courtney, happily returning home for the school holidays. Her eyes sought the corner room on the first floor which had been hers in a swift surge of nostalgia. She had the oddest feeling that if she could look in through the uncurtained window, it would all be waiting for her there, totally unchanged, with the little davenport under the window, and the girl's bed with its flowered and flounced coverlet, and the elegant pieces of walnut furniture all chosen for her by her father.

Courtney sighed swiftly. She was just being a fool. All the furniture had been sold long ago. There was nothing left at Hunters Court to remind her of the girl she had been, or the secure life she had enjoyed. She had managed to salvage one thing—her mother's portrait which had always hung on the wide half-landing at the bend of the stairs. It was too large for her bedroom at the cottage where it now hung, and it was

like living with an older version of herself which could
be disconcerting at times. She barely remembered her
mother who had died when she was three, and she had
only recently become aware how like her she was—the
same oval face, framed by the same cloud of dark hair,
except that Courtney wore hers slightly smoother, and
definitely longer—the same slightly tilted grey-green
eyes, with the long dark lashes. Courtney often felt she
had never felt the loss of her mother so keenly as in the
past few years. She could have done with that serenity,
the curve of humour in the well-shaped mouth. She
needed someone to turn to, and Rob required someone
to exercise some control over him, whether he knew it
or not. Their father was too ill, and although there had
been improvement over the past few months, they had
to be careful not to agitate him.

Presumably Rob had taken this into account when he
told him of the plan for Hunters Court, or at least
Courtney hoped he had. She doubted all the same
whether Rob would have been completely frank with
his father. He could not imagine that James Lincoln
would welcome the wholesale changes which would be
bound to follow once Monty Pallister owned the
property.

She parked the car at the front of the house and
walked slowly up the shallow flight of steps which led
to the terrace. The windows seemed to look down at her
like reproachful eyes, and she concentrated on looking
over the maintenance of the house with eagle eyes. But
she couldn't fault it. Paintwork, guttering and roof
seemed to be in perfect order. There were bulbs
showing faint green tips in the large ornamental urns
along the terrace, and Courtney wondered whether they
would ever have a chance to flower. Then she caught at
herself impatiently. There was no point in thinking
along these lines. She had come here to encapsulate
some memories, not indulge in useless recriminations.

She tried the doors and french windows as she
passed, but they were all securely locked, and in a way
she was relieved. If there had been some means of

ingress, the temptation would probably have proved too strong, and she had to come to terms with the fact that there was nothing left for her here.

A sudden chill breeze had sprung up, mocking the sunshine, and she turned up the collar of her sheepskin coat with a slight shiver as she descended the terrace steps at the side of the house and walked, her boot heels scrunching on the neatly raked gravel, along the path towards the gardens at the rear. There was a short cut through the yard which housed the stables and garaging, and she decided to take that, but as she turned under the arch, she saw something which brought her up short. There was a car parked there, a silver-grey Porsche. Courtney stared at it, frowning a little. It wasn't a local registration, she noted, and yet the driver knew enough to find his way to the parking area at the rear rather than leave it at the front as she had done. She grimaced. Possibly Monty, or one of his minions, had arrived for one last gloat before the auction. Monty usually drove an opulent Jaguar, but that didn't mean it was his only car.

She glanced around uneasily. She had as much right to be here as anyone else, but she hoped that if it was Monty, he hadn't seen her. She had managed up to now to present a façade of civility, but now she knew exactly what he wanted, she wasn't sure that the lessons of her upbringing would stand. And while she opposed Rob, she wasn't prepared to jeopardise his position by openly quarrelling with the man who was going to employ him.

She hurried across the yard, and unlatched the gate which led into the gardens. It squeaked loudly, and she winced, expecting to hear herself challenged. But there wasn't another sound, and she made herself relax.

Whoever was there, they were more likely to be looking round the house than the grounds. They'd have borrowed the keys from the agents, and probably decided to use the rear entrance as it was more convenient.

Nevertheless, she found she was hurrying, and moving as quietly as possible, just as though she was some kind of intruder, and she was frankly relieved when she reached the comparative shelter of the rose garden. Looking at the beds of leafless bushes, it seemed impossible to imagine the riot of colour that only the passage of a few months would bring. She wandered down the paths between the beds, pausing to read some of the labels and refresh her memory with a scent—a colour. She wondered if any of them would be transplanted, or whether they would simply be yanked out and burnt.

Her steps slowed as she reached the sheltered corner where the exquisite damask and moss roses grew. Surely they could be preserved? Or were they too going to be sacrificed in the wholesale vandalism that Monty Pallister threatened for Hunters Court? She felt a sharp sting of tears, and at the same moment her senses, heightened perhaps by emotional stress, told her that she was no longer alone. She heard the scrunch of another step on the gravel behind her.

Damnation! she thought furiously. It was humiliating to be found here, crying over a lot of flower beds, especially if it was Monty who had found her.

She turned unwillingly, bracing herself, then stopped dead, the defensive phrases she'd been planning escaping her lips in one startled gasp.

The man confronting her was not plump and sleekly upholstered, with an oily smile. He was tall with tawny hair, and hazel eyes, and there was a scar high on his cheekbone where once there had been a trickle of blood. And he wasn't smiling at all.

CHAPTER TWO

HE wasn't a ghost, he was flesh and blood, but no apparition could have frightened her more.

He said, 'So we meet again, Courtney.'

He said it without emotion, just a flat recognition of the fact that time and fate had conspired to bring them together, but the words seemed to tear at her like long ago thorns.

Her voice sounded thick. 'What are you doing here?'

He shrugged. 'I was in the area, and I heard someone say the place was back on the market. I thought I'd have a look round for old times' sake.'

Breathing was painful, but she fought for her control. His cold, speculative gaze seemed to be warning her that he had not forgotten their last meeting, and as if to reinforce this impression, his hand rose and touched the little scar.

He said softly, 'And you, Courtney? What brings you back here? A trip down memory lane?'

The question was bland enough, but there was something in the way he said it, something about the way his eyes narrowed slightly which alerted her suspicions.

He'd said he was in the area, which sounded casual enough—and yet ... Three years ago he had vanished out of their lives completely, and now, when Hunters Court was for sale again, he was back. Was it just a coincidence? Surely it must be, yet the Porsche suggested affluence, as did the dark supple leather of the car coat which hung from his shoulders, and the rollneck cashmere sweater beneath it.

She made herself speak lightly. 'Pure nostalgia, I'm afraid, which is invariably a mistake. I didn't expect to find anyone else here.'

His brows rose sardonically. 'No? A desirable

residence like this? I would have thought there'd have been a queue forming.'

Courtney smiled brightly. 'Perhaps there is. I wouldn't know.'

Her mind seemed to be running in circles like a mouse on a wheel. There was a growing conviction within her that Blair's questions were only casual on the surface. But surely he, of all people, could not seriously be interested in buying Hunters Court. She was just being over-imaginative. She had to be. Because the thought of Blair Devereux, the nephew of the man who had ruined her father, living in her old home was even more intolerable than Monty Pallister's plans for the house.

'But all the same, you wouldn't keep away.' Blair was smiling too, but the smile hadn't reached his eyes. 'It's not really surprising, I suppose. After all those generations of Lincolns living here, the place must have the pull of a magnet for you all.'

'Perhaps,' she said. 'But it isn't ours any more, and I don't forget that.'

She was issuing a warning of her own, reminding him of everything which lay between them, the abyss which the sordid aftermath of betrayal and embezzlement had created. The girl whom he'd teased with a summer kiss in this very garden no longer existed. She was older now and infinitely more wary. For a short while, she had allowed herself to forget that she didn't really like Blair Devereux because she had been frankly dazzled by his sexual magnetism, but that would never happen again.

Yet it didn't stop her wanting to remove herself from his orbit with the speed of light. Apart from anything else she had an uneasy feeling that she ought to get back to the cottage and tell Rob what had happened. He wouldn't be happy to know that Blair was back in the vicinity, even if it was only a brief visit.

He was always bad news, she thought, and he won't have changed.

She summoned the bright smile again. 'Well, I must be going. I have a lot to do this morning.'

'Is that a fact?' He consulted an expensive-looking gold wristwatch. 'I was thinking perhaps we could have lunch together.'

She was taken aback at that. He had unmitigated gall even to suggest such a thing, she thought furiously. He was the last person she'd ever wanted to meet again, and she'd have thought he felt exactly the same about her.

She said calmly, 'I'm afraid not.'

'Then how about dinner? I'm staying at the White Hart.'

Courtney stiffened slightly. That was more bad news. She'd hoped he was just passing through. 'Impossible, I'm afraid.'

'Clearly you're a busy lady.'

And what did he think? That she'd spent the last three years sitting like faithful Penelope waiting for him to come back? She wanted to laugh in his face, but if he was prepared to maintain this veneer of civilised conversation, then so would she.

She said, 'I manage to keep occupied. Well, goodbye, Blair. I hope you enjoy the rest of your—holiday.'

'It's certainly begun well.' He smiled slightly. 'It's always pleasant to meet old friends.'

Friends? she wanted to shout at him. We were never friends. And now we're enemies, and you know it.

The last time they had met she had screamed her hatred at him. There had been no smiles and civilised words then. They had been adversaries, and the scar was proof. And instinct told her that they were adversaries still.

She had to walk past him to reach the gate, for a moment she held her breath as if he might put out a hand and take hold of her. If he did, then all the smiles and polite nothings would shatter like glass, and she would fight him like a tigress. He would have other scars to add to his collection, but of course, he didn't try and touch her, and she felt herself give an infinitesimal sigh of relief as she reached the gate.

She half-turned, lifting a hand in acknowledgment

and farewell, and Blair said softly, 'Remember me to your family.'

Just for a moment he let the mask drop, and she was appalled at the expression she saw in his eyes. Whatever he'd come there for, it wasn't to build any bridges, and she was scared. Geoffrey Devereux was dead, and her father was an invalid, and she'd thought that the worst that could happen was over, but now she wasn't so sure.

She walked back to the car, trying not to run because he might be watching, and her heart was thudding, and her palms felt clammy. The routine of starting the car helped steady her a little, and when she finally emerged on to the road she turned in the opposite direction away from the village, and drove for about a mile before pulling off into a parking space.

She switched off the ignition and wound down the window, breathing slowly and deeply, relishing the scent of the crisp clean air. Any notion she might have had that Blair was making overtures because he wanted to forgive and forget had been laid to rest for ever.

It was a ludicrous situation, because by any reckoning, her family were the injured parties in the whole tragic, sordid business. But Blair had never seemed to take that into account. She clasped her hands on the steering wheel and leaned her forehead on them.

Blair had come to Hunters Court that night to demand that Geoffrey Devereux be given bail. Looking back, she could understand his motive. He must have known that his uncle had a weak heart, and that the upset of being in custody could endanger him, but what she could not forgive was that he seemed to blame her father for not wishing to intervene. Blair clearly felt that if James Lincoln offered to put up the bail for his erstwhile partner, then the police might drop their opposition, and when her father was unwilling, he had exploded into near-violence.

Courtney shivered as she remembered that terrible evening. She had been drawn to the study by the sound of raised voices, and when she had gone in, had found herself in the middle of a confrontation.

There had been all kinds of raw and savage emotion in the air, and although she hadn't completely understood it all, she'd been frightened nevertheless, and quick to spring to her father's defence. Because he wasn't making a very good job out of defending himself, just sitting in his chair while Blair stood over him, his whole attitude one of naked aggression.

Courtney had interposed herself between them, glaring at Blair. 'Who let you in here? What do you want?'

'I want my uncle out of that stinking jail,' he muttered between his teeth. 'And I've come to—persuade his closest friend to help.'

James Lincoln said in a faint voice, 'How can I? the police . . .'

'To hell with that,' Blair had said in the same soft chilling tone he'd used when he said *'Remember me to your family'* 'You can make them listen to you, and by heaven, you will, if you know what's good for you.'

'How dare you threaten my father!' Courtney was disgusted to hear how young and breathless she sounded.

'Because the real threat's to my uncle.' He hardly looked at her. All his attention was concentrated on the pale-faced man in the chair in front of him. 'For heaven's sake, man, you can't let this happen to him. He's your friend!'

'Friend?' Courtney intervened fiercely when James Lincoln remained silent. 'A fine friend he's been! He's lied to us, and cheated and stolen. He deserves to be in jail!'

Blair gave her a contemptuous look. 'You don't know what you're talking about,' he said shortly. 'So you'd better keep quiet. This is between your father and myself.' He turned back to James Lincoln. 'Now are you coming with me to put up bail for him willingly, or do I have to make you?'

He seemed to loom towards them, and Courtney saw her father shrink. She snatched at a heavy crystal ashtray on the desk in front of her and threw it at Blair. He moved sharply to avoid it, but one corner caught him a glancing glow on the cheekbone, and he swore violently.

She said, 'He's not going anywhere with you, Blair Devereux, and if you don't leave the house, I'm going to call the police, and you'll find that you're in jail as well as your uncle!'

He looked past her at James Lincoln. He said harshly, 'You could be condemning him to death. You realise that—and yet you're still not prepared to do anything.'

James Lincoln said again, 'I can't . . .' and his voice faded as if he was exhausted.

The talk of death scared Courtney, and her voice rose hysterically. 'Get out of here—get out! Leave us alone! Haven't you done enough harm? Can't you see he's ill?'

And his final damning reply, 'He deserves to be ill—and more.'

She raised her head, shuddering inwardly. In her secret heart, she'd always blamed Blair for bringing that stroke on her father. He'd been shattered by the realisation that his partner had become a criminal, but he would have come round. He would have made good the losses and survived and carried on. But that scene with Blair had destroyed him, and he was never the same again. And the news that Geoffrey Devereux had succumbed to a heart attack in his cell had proved the final intolerable straw.

Courtney wondered if Blair knew about her father's stroke. She could imagine him receiving the news with a kind of grim satisfaction, and he would have reacted to the information that the Lincolns had lost their home and everything they possessed in the aftermath in exactly the same way. He blamed them for his uncle's death, as if in some way it conferred a posthumous innocence. He seemed to forget that nothing could justify the kind of injury Geoffrey Devereux had done them all. His death had been tragic, but he was in jail because he deserved to be, and Blair Devereux had had no right—no right at all, to try and bully her father into mitigating the course of justice. It was cruel of him, she thought passionately.

But then he was cruel. She had never doubted it even for that brief time when he had shown her some tenderness. Because that had been calculated from the beginning, although she was unable to understand his motives. Probably it was simply because she had always been impervious to his undoubted charm, and this had piqued him. He was a predator, pure and simple, although she would never have described Blair Devereux as either pure or simple.

She heard the sound of a horn, and jerking upright, she saw the Porsche drive past, and Blair lift a mocking hand in imitation of her own attempted casual goodbye.

Damn him, she thought. She had driven this way in order to avoid him, because she thought he would be going back to the White Hart, and now he'd seen her skulking in this layby, and who only knew what conclusions he would draw from that, but they would probably be quite correct.

And now she had to drive back to the village and speak to Robin, when all she really wanted to do was find somewhere to hide. Which was ridiculous, because she had nothing to fear from Blair. He was the one who should be avoiding them, which made his unexpected return even more troubling. For the past three years she had tried to convince herself that he was part of a bad dream. Well, she was wide awake now and all her senses were jumping. The bird of ill omen had returned, and there could be storm clouds gathering on the horizon even now.

Robin was talking on the phone when she arrived back, and when he replaced the receiver he looked almost jaunty, and she was sorry she had to dispel his optimistic mood.

She said without preamble, 'Blair Devereux was at the house just now. I thought you should know.'

'Blair?' His voice rose incredulously, and he stared at her. 'What the hell did he want? What did he say?'

She shrugged. 'Not a great deal, but he made me—uneasy.' And that was putting it mildly, she thought wryly.

Robin looked rigid with dismay. 'And he was at the house. Did—did he seem interested in it? Does he know it's for sale?'

'Of course. He'd have hardly been wandering around if the Hallorans had been in residence.'

Robin gestured impatiently. 'I mean—does he know the auction's tomorrow?'

'I've no idea. I certainly didn't tell him.' Courtney eyed him measuringly, wishing that she had said nothing. He looked as if he was going to be sick.

Robin chewed at his lip. 'Is he still at Hunters Court?'

Courtney shook her head. 'No, he left just after me. He's staying at the White Hart,' she added.

Robin groaned. 'God, that's all I need! Then he does know about the auction.'

'It's hardly a State secret.' She was trying to make him smile. 'There'll be other people there beside you. It's a public auction.'

Rob said miserably, 'I know that—but he's one member of the public I could do without.'

'But you can't stop him going,' she pointed out. 'And he can't be that interested or he'd have got the key from Paxton's.'

'What would he need to see?' Robin demanded. 'He knows that house almost as well as we do.'

'That's true.' Courtney drew a deep breath. 'Rob, I just can't believe it. Why should he want Hunters Court? It makes no sense.'

He said heavily, 'Envy. Bitterness. I can think of a list of reasons. You didn't know him as well as I did in the old days.'

'I didn't want to know him,' she said drily. 'But I find envy hard to swallow. Why should he envy us?'

'I don't know much about his background,' said Robin. 'But I do know there wasn't much money. That was probably why he attached himself to dear Uncle

Geoffrey, and through him to us. And he certainly made himself at home each time he came. He used to spend hours in the library reading up on the history of the place. If we'd ever decided to do conducted tours, we could have hired Blair as a guide. He knew more about it than Dad, and he probably convinced himself that he cared more than any of us. Of course he wants it.'

Courtney said slowly, 'You said there wasn't much money. But I think there is now.' She described the car, his clothes, the handmade Italian shoes, and Robin's eyes grew hard and angry.

'Well, we don't need to ask where he got it from.' Courtney looked at him blankly, and he went on, 'The police never found out what Geoffrey Devereux did with the money he stole. If they had, we might still be living at Hunters Court ourselves.'

She gasped. 'You're not serious! You're saying that *Blair* has the money?'

'It makes sense. Someone has to have it, and he seems to have changed into a have from a have-not in the last three years. What was he officially? A mining surveyor? Hardly enough to put him in the millionaire bracket.'

'Unless he found his own private goldmine.'

Robin looked at her grimly. 'With our gold in it.'

Courtney sank down on a chair, feeling numb. 'It's not possible—is it?'

'Anything's possible,' Robin said bitterly. 'He's been out of the picture ever since Geoffrey Devereux died, and if anyone had a clue as to where the money was, it would be him. And money makes money. He's probably put his absence to good use.'

She shook her head. 'He'd need to if he wants to buy Hunters Court, but I still can't believe that he does.'

She didn't want to believe it. She'd resented Blair, for all kinds of reasons, some of which she hadn't been able to define too clearly, when he was only a visitor. But the thought of him as owner—possessor, moving among those well-loved rooms, filled her with a sick distaste. She thought she would rather see the place burned to the ground, or wrecked by Monty Pallister, than watch it fall into Blair's hands.

She said, half to herself, 'There's nothing we can do.'

'Yes, there is,' Robin said forcefully. 'We can find out exactly what he's up to. You say he's at the White Hart—well, we'll have dinner there this evening.'

Courtney looked at him, then quickly shook her head. 'No—I can't. I don't want to.'

'It's not a question of what you want.' Robin's mouth twisted. 'Do you think I want to see him again? Of all the people in the world ... ' He gave a little cracked laugh. 'But it's got to be done. Too much hangs on this deal. No Devereux is going to ruin any more of my life.'

'Brave words,' she said ironically. 'But even if Blair confides in you, and he's going to the auction tomorrow, what can you do to stop him?'

'I'll think of something. And you'll help.'

Courtney shook her head again. 'That's quite impossible. Anyway, I'm seeing Clive this evening.'

'Oh—Clive,' said Robin with dissatisfaction, and his sister gave him a swift glance.

He had never totally approved of her seeing Clive FitzHugh, and up to quite recently this had not particularly bothered her because it was a casual relationship created more by familiarity and proximity than searing passion. They'd known each other since they were children, and in the last twelve months had drifted into each other's company for trips to the cinema and theatre in the surrounding large towns, and sometimes they sampled the local eating houses. Clive was only Robin's age, and certainly not ready to settle down into thoughts of marriage, which was a relief to Courtney, who knew that although Colonel and Mrs FitzHugh were always kindness itself, they would not welcome the idea of their son tying himself up to a penniless girl. The FitzHughs had always been local landowners and they were nowhere near the breadline, but they would expect Clive to marry 'sensibly' in the fullness of time. Meanwhile they welcomed Courtney into their home in much the same spirit as they had done when she was a child. Courtney herself was well content with the relationship. Clive was good company, if nothing more, and the area of Harlow St Mary wasn't overflowing with young bachelors eager and willing to take her out.

Clive and she were going out for a meal that evening, and she wasn't prepared to put him off to pursue some wildcat scheme of Robin's. Besides, she didn't want to have to see Blair Devereux again.

It was an unfortunate sort of day, and more than once she wished she was at the office. She could have found something to do there surely, and it would have been better than listening to Robin's constant jeremiads. Uncle Philip telephoned during the afternoon—to find out if Robin was ever going to work at the bank again, Courtney surmised. She absented herself tactfully for the duration of the call, but the cottage was too small to avoid altogether Robin's voice raised in complaint and self-justification, and although she could only hear his side of the conversation, it was clear it was not going his way.

He offered no explanations when she rejoined him, but there was something about the set of his shoulders, and the mutinous expression on his face which spoke volumes. She guessed that if not actually dismissed, he had certainly been given some kind of ultimatum, and wondered what else he could have expected.

It was a relief to have her date with Clive to prepare for. To be able to lock herself in the tiny bathroom and pamper herself with bath oil, and scented powder. She put on a red needlecord skirt, softly full from a tight waistband, and a white blouse, ruffled at the neck and cuffs. She highlighted her eyes and cheekbones, and put a warm gloss on her mouth. When she had finished, she was quietly satisfied, having few illusions about her own cool attraction.

When she went down to the living room to wait for

Clive, she found Robin had already left, and she couldn't be sorry.

Clive arrived punctually, his blue eyes holding a smiling admiration as he looked at her.

'You look positively edible,' he told her. 'I'm sorry we aren't going somewhere more exotic.'

Courtney's heart sank at his words, but she concealed it.

'Where are we going?' she asked brightly.

'I booked a table at the White Hart for eight o'clock,' said Clive, glancing at his watch. 'I thought we could have a drink somewhere else first.'

'Marvellous!' Courtney kept her smile firmly pinned in place. She could only hope silently that Robin had had second thoughts about seeking Blair out. Perhaps neither of them would be there, she thought, crossing her fingers surreptitiously in the folds of her skirt. She resolved to take as long as possible over the preliminary drink, in order to give them a chance to meet and go their separate ways before she and Clive arrived on the scene.

But when they walked into the small cocktail bar at the White Hart some three-quarters of an hour later, Courtney realised that none of her hopes were to be fulfilled.

Blair was sitting with Robin at a corner table. Rob looked up as she walked in, and although he smiled at her and waved, the expression in his eyes said trouble.

Clive said, surprised, 'You didn't tell me old Rob was going to be here tonight. And who's that he's with. It looks like ...' He paused abruptly, obviously embarrassed.

Courtney said rather tautly, 'I didn't tell you because I didn't know. And you're quite right about his companion—it is Blair Devereux.'

She didn't want to join them. There were other tables, but both men had risen and were waiting, so unwillingly she crossed the bar.

'What an unexpected pleasure,' Blair said smilingly. 'First Rob, and now you, Courtney. This is turning into quite a reunion.'

'Yes, isn't it.' She kept her tone light. 'You'll have to excuse us. We're dining here and . . .'

'Oh, I haven't eaten yet either,' Blair said calmly, and he signalled towards the head waiter who was hovering in the doorway of the dining room. 'I hope that you'll join me as my guests.'

Clive was looking totally baffled by the entire situation, and never more so than when Courtney tucked her hand through his arm.

'We couldn't do that,' she said. 'They say three's a crowd, so four is plainly impossible. I'm sure you understand.'

'I do indeed,' said Blair. 'Nevertheless I hope you'll change your mind.'

Robin broke in. 'Yes, come and join us, you two. After all, it's not often that such old friends have a chance to get together again.' He shot Courtney a veiled, urgent look.

Clive said feebly, 'Look, I just don't know about this. I'd rather counted on having Courtney all to myself this evening.'

'But you can see her any time,' Robin argued. 'Come on, Clive, be a sport!'

Courtney was still prepared to argue, but she sensed that their discussion was attracting some curious glances from other parts of the room, and the head waiter, all smiles, was bearing down on them with menus and wine lists, so she reluctantly acceded. To her dismay she found she was being ushered to the wide velvet-covered bench seat which ran the length of the wall to sit beside Blair. She smoothed her skirt round her slim legs, taking care that the folds went nowhere near him, then put her bag on the seat between them, knowing by the faint smile playing around his mouth that he was quite well aware of her manoeuvres.

But she was past caring what he thought. It was no wish of hers to be here. It had been brought about by an ironic combination of circumstances She had hoped never to see him again.

She stole a look at Clive. He knew perfectly well what the situation was, and must be wondering what Robin was doing on such apparently friendly terms with someone who, in ordinary circumstances, would have been regarded as an enemy. He knew too that there had been no contact at all between the Lincolns and the remaining family of their former business partner for several years. And Clive wasn't the only one to be puzzled. There were other local people and acquaintances in the room who would be watching avidly, intrigued by this unexpected piece of gossip.

She ordered melon and a rare *filet mignon* almost at random. Her appetite had vanished anyway. Across the table Rob was talking slightly too loudly and laughing rather too much, and she winced inwardly. It was the kind of performance calculated to put Blair Devereux on his guard. He certainly wasn't all chatter and *bonhomie*. On the contrary, the expression on his face was almost sardonic.

If Rob goes on like this, he's going to run out of topics before the first course is served, Courtney thought, adding mercilessly—and he needn't expect me to help him out!

It was easier in a way once they got into the dining room and the food was being served. Its excellence was a perfectly acceptable conversational gambit, and even Clive joined in with some relief.

'I'd forgotten how good English food could be,' Blair commented.

'Oh?' Clive looked at him. 'Have you been abroad?'

As Blair nodded, Rob asked breezily, 'Anywhere interesting?'

'A whole number of places,' Blair drawled. 'But I'm sure you don't need a travelogue from me.'

Ah, but you're wrong, Courtney said silently. I'd like to know where you've been. I wonder if Switzerland was on the itinerary, and whether you've now got one of those famous numbered accounts as a souvenir.

He was watching her across the flicker of the candles on the table. He said softly, 'But you, Courtney—

what's been happening to you? You vanished so rapidly this morning, I didn't get a chance to ask. You were planning an academic future of some kind, if my memory serves.'

Her smile became stretched and tight. 'Oh, that didn't transpire,' she said. 'I'm a working girl.'

'Interesting job?' There was something in his expression which warned her that he already knew where she worked and exactly what her employment comprised.

She said calmly, 'Fascinating,' and ate her last sliver of melon as if it actually tasted like succulent fruit instead of ashes in her mouth.

He watched her for a moment, his smile widening, then he said gently, 'And Rob, I hear, is becoming quite something in the City.'

'I'm glad you think so.' Briefly, Rob let his mask of geniality slip. 'I'd have described it as a dead-end job myself.'

Blair's brows rose. 'I hardly think Monty Pallister would be pleased to hear an assocation with him described in such unflattering terms.' His voice was soft.

Courtney silently thanked Providence for the waiter who appeared at that moment to clear the table and bring the next course. The minor upheaval provided Rob with a breathing space.

At last he said with a fair measure of poise, 'I think you've been misinformed. Mr Pallister is unlikely to be interested in a nonentity like me.'

'You don't do yourself justice,' Blair said lightly. 'I understand the gentleman in question is always on the look-out for fresh talent to help him in his— endeavours.' The pause was smooth and quite deliberate, as Courtney knew was the choice of word. She stared down at her plate as if she was trying to analyse the lyonnais potatoes which lay there.

Clive broke in. 'Changing your job, old boy? You've never mentioned anything about it.'

'Because there's nothing to mention.' Robin's laugh

was uneasy. 'I like their way of doing calabrese here, don't you?'

'Very much,' Blair agreed evenly. 'In fact I'm so impressed with the place as a whole, I'm tempted to extend my stay.'

There was a brief pause, then Clive said, 'Fantastic. Then we can hope to see more of you?'

'Oh, yes,' Blair said gravely, 'I think I can safely promise that.' His face was expressionless as he glanced at Courtney, but at the back of his eyes little devils of amusement danced as if he knew the effect it was costing her to use the knife in her hand on the steak instead of himself.

Rob rallied, concealing his dismay. 'Well, Courtney has a few days off from work. I'm sure she'd be glad to help you rediscover old haunts.'

For a moment she couldn't believe what she'd just heard. She stared at Rob, an indignant denial already forming on her lips, then she saw the urgent appeal in his eyes and subsided in silence. Her mind was whirling frantically. What in the world was Rob playing at? He couldn't imagine that she wanted to spend one more second in Blair Devereux's company than she had to, especially after this horrendous meal. Yet she couldn't ignore that silent plea from him, even though she didn't understand it.

Blair said, 'I was thinking of a run over to Hylam Abbey tomorrow, if the weather stays fine. Would you come with me, Courtney?'

She made her tone casual. 'I'm not sure what my plans are for tomorrow yet, I'm afraid. Isn't it a bit early in the year for exploring ruins?'

'I thought nostalgia was a warming sentiment,' Blair said lightly. 'However, just as you please.'

It would have pleased her very much to tell him to go to hell, she thought, but for Rob's sake she had at least been civil.

And Hylam Abbey was one of her favourite places. The grey tumbled stones beside the smooth, slow weaving of the river had been a solace to her so often.

The thought of sharing them with Blair Devereux was a kind of desecration.

The sweet trolley came round with its usual cargo of cream-drenched goodies, but Courtney refused them, asking simply for a coffee.

She turned to Clive, putting a hand on his sleeve. 'Could we go fairly soon, darling? I've got a brute of a headache.'

He looked surprised and gratified at the unexpected endearment, and the beguiling warmth of her smile and gesture. 'Of course.' He looked at Robin. 'Can we give you a lift?'

'No, thanks.' Robin shook his head. 'I think I'll hang on for some more coffee and perhaps another brandy.'

Courtney wondered whether she ought to give him a word of warning. He had already drunk plenty of the excellent wine Blair had ordered to be served, and he had no real head for alcohol. But she guessed there was little point in any intervention from her. He would be too annoyed that she had resisted Blair's invitation to heed it.

The waiter came to draw back her chair, and they all rose when she did and walked to the archway which led into the bar, Blair pausing to give orders for fresh coffee and the brandies to be served there. There was a slight skirmish over the bill which Blair won, and Courtney felt annoyance rise in her at his self-assurance. She wished Clive had been more insistent. She didn't want to be beholden to Blair for the food she had just eaten.

The story about the headache wasn't a total lie. There was a throbbing sensation behind her temples, induced by stress, she had little doubt.

They stood in the bar and she hoped her smile didn't look as insincere as it felt as she said, 'Well, thank you for a very pleasant evening. Enjoy your stay.'

'I'm sure I shall,' said Blair. 'Take care of that headache,' he added softly, and he moved, his hand lifting as if he was going to touch her face, stroke the curve of her cheek.

Her reaction was immediate and violent; she stepped backwards out of range and collided with Clive as she did so. She had to apologise, of course, claiming that she had stumbled, and blaming her high heel, but she saw from the irony on Blair's face that he had not been deceived for an instant.

She wanted to say to Robin, 'Whatever you're doing, whatever you're going to say to him—be careful! But she didn't. The whole situation was beyond her, and Robin would have to look out for himself. She was thankful to be going home.

But that wasn't all plain sailing either. Clive had taken her eagerness to go home as an indication that she wanted their relationship to move on a stage or two, and she needed all the diplomacy at her command to evade him, and his excited, seeking hands and mouth, and convince him that she really was tired, and her headache now a positive reality. He was clearly disappointed but still docile, and as she shut the cottage door, she was thankful for his gentlemanly upbringing. All the same, this new development might mean the end of the relationship, she thought with mild regret as she mixed herself a soluble aspirin and swallowed it with a slight shudder. She had enjoyed their outings, but she wanted no deeper commitment than that, nothing that might hold an element of courtship. It was her own fault if there was a change in his attitude. She had adopted a more flirtatious attitude towards him all evening quite deliberately, even though she wasn't quite sure what had motivated her to do so. A desire to impress on Blair Devereux that she was no longer the child he had once known? She hoped not. Heaven help her if any of her actions was designed to impress him in any way!

It was cold in her bedroom, but she resisted the impulse to turn on the small fan-heater. Even a small cottage like this seemed to eat electricity, and she was responsible for paying the quarterly bills, so she tried to exercise some care.

She sighed as she got into bed. How different

everything had been once. And how much she had taken for granted. She doubted whether she had ever given a moment's thought to the size of the electricity bill at Hunters Court.

What a pampered selfish little bitch I must have been, she thought, huddling the covers round her.

The aspirin did its work after a while, but sleep remained oddly elusive. Courtney supposed that subconsciously she was waiting for Rob to come home, although it was unlikely that he would disturb her unless she left her light on, and she wasn't prepared to do that.

She didn't want to hear any more about Blair Devereux or Rob's fears and suspicions. It was disturbing and unfortunate that he'd turned up when he did, but it was a coincidence, no more than that. It had to be. It probably gave him satisfaction to embarrass them, and let them think he had been keeping tabs on them all this time. At the same time, she couldn't help wondering just how Blair had known about Robin's association with Monty Pallister.

She burrowed her cheek into the pillow, determinedly closing her eyes. Perhaps by tomorrow the fine weather would have fled, and there would be a blizzard. She couldn't imagine Blair wanting to hang about under those circumstances.

She murmured drowsily, 'Please, let it hail or snow.' And on that pious request, she fell asleep.

The first thing she realised as she drew back her curtains the following morning was that her prayers had not been granted. There were a few clouds about, but none of them threatened anything worse than the lightest of showers, and all in all it promised to be another fine day.

Courtney pulled on jeans and a sweater and made her way downstairs to the living room. As she pushed open the door, she heard the sound of the telephone receiver being replaced, and realised to her surprise that Robin was already up. He wasn't a notably early riser when he was at the cottage, and he couldn't be afraid of missing the auction because the time was only nine o'clock, and the sale wasn't due to begin until midday.

She said teasingly, 'Did your hangover keep you awake? Can I make you some breakfast, or would black coffee . . .' She broke off, because she had just seen his face as he turned slowly towards her, and he looked pale, drawn, even haunted.

She said, 'Rob, what is it? Who was on the phone? It isn't Daddy? He's not...'

'What?' He looked at her almost blankly, then recovered. 'No, of course not. I thought when you saw him last there'd been an improvement.'

'A slight one,' she admitted. 'But that doesn't mean much at all, apparently. Well, what is it, then?'

He sat down. He said hoarsely, 'I—I rang Monty. I thought he should know about Devereux being in the area, and what I suspected.' He swallowed. 'He wasn't pleased.'

Courtney studied him for a moment, then sat down beside him. 'Don't you think that was a little foolish? After all, you've no proof that Blair wants the house. Why disturb—your friend unnecessarily?'

'Because he ordered me to tell him if anyone seemed to be showing even the slightest interest,' Robin said shortly. 'I talked to Devereux for ages after you'd gone last night, and I still couldn't get anything out of him. But he's up to something. He must be. He has no reason to love us, and this certainly isn't the ideal season for a holiday in the English countryside. But he's like a clam when he wants to be.' He moistened his lips with his tongue. 'I wish I could be sure that he was out of the way until the auction was safely over.'

'Well, he said he was going to Hylam Abbey,' Courtney reminded him reasonably. 'The weather's perfect, so that's probably what he'll do.'

'But I can't be sure.' Robin's unhappy gaze sought hers. 'Monty hit the roof when he heard his name had come into the conversation. He accused me of talking out of turn—he wouldn't let me explain.'

Courtney felt a stirring of compassion for her brother, but at the same time she couldn't help a secret pleasure if the seeds of disillusion with Monty Pallister were being sown. She'd never felt that it was an association which would benefit Robin ultimately.

'Well, is it a State secret?' She strove for a light tone.

'It's damn near—or it was intended to be. All successful businessmen have enemies. There are a lot of people who'd like to beat Monty at his own game. That's why he hired me to front for him. Blair could be fronting for someone too.'

Courtney sighed under her breath. Rob really did look ghastly. Almost frightened, except that would be ridiculous.

'Perhaps Mr Pallister has never yet learned the valuable lesson that you can't win them all,' she said. 'It wouldn't be the end of the world if he was beaten at the auction, you know.'

'That's what you think,' Robin muttered. 'He's made it only too clear that he doesn't expect me to be beaten. I have to win at all costs.' He groaned. 'He's invested in Hunters Court already—a lot of time, and a lot of money. He doesn't intend his investment to go down the drain.' He stared at her. 'Courtney, I'm pinning my hopes on the fact that Devereux only arrived here yesterday. He didn't tell me that, but I checked in the hotel register. He may know the house is for sale, but if he hasn't been to the agents' he may not know when the auction's being held.'

'No, he probably doesn't, but it wouldn't take him long to find out,' Courtney returned rather drily. 'Rob, calm down. I think we're making mountains out of molehills here. It's my fault—I overreacted when I saw Blair, but I've had time to think now, and I can't believe . . .'

Robin said, 'I can't take that chance.' He leaned forward. 'You've got to help me, Courtney. You've got to keep him out of the way until the sale's safely over.'

She looked at him in total disbelief. 'And how am I

supposed to do that? Kidnap him? Oh, Rob, you can't be serious!'

'I've never been more so,' he said in a low voice. 'Courtney, you must help. It means everything to me. If Monty doesn't buy Hunters Court, the consequences could be disastrous.'

'Not for Hunters Court they wouldn't be.' Courtney tried to make a joke of it, but the expression on Robin's face had set alarm bells ringing. 'Don't you think you're over-dramatising the situation? What would be the worst that could happen? That Monty Pallister would withdraw his offer? Well, I'm sure Uncle Philip would have you back. Or, if you didn't want that, perhaps we could both move somewhere else and make a fresh start. There's always something . . .'

Robin shook his head. 'No—you don't realise,' he muttered. 'It isn't as simple as that. There's money involved.'

'Don't tell me he couldn't write it off as a tax loss,' Courtney said contemptuously. 'I'm sure Mr Pallister knows all those kind of angles.'

Robin's hands were tightly clenched in front of him. 'He advanced some money to me,' he said. 'As a kind of retainer, I suppose. Half then, and the remainder when Hunters Court was his.' He swallowed. 'He warned me, just now, that if anything goes wrong, I'll have to repay him—and I can't.'

Courtney stared at him, totally dismayed. 'How much money?' she asked shakily at last, and when he told her, she gasped in consternation.

'You can't have spent it.'

He shook his head. 'Not exactly. I—I was in debt to begin with, and Monty offered to help out. That was how it all began really.'

'What kind of debt?' It was like a nightmare.

He said sullenly, 'There was this club—I used to gamble there. I had to have more money, Courtney. I couldn't manage properly on what Uncle Philip paid, and I won at first. I won quite a lot. Then—it all started to go wrong.' He glanced up at her. He looked very young and frightened, and she felt a thousand years old.

'And how did Monty Pallister come into all this?' she asked.

Robin shrugged. 'I suppose—he owns the club.'

'There's no supposition about it,' she said. 'Oh, Rob, you fool!'

He bit his lip. 'Don't start on me, Courtney. You can't say anything to make me feel worse than I do. He called it a gentleman's agreement. It all seemed—well, foolproof, at the time.'

'I'm sure it did,' she said bitterly. 'What a pity it didn't also seem immoral—your old home for some gambling debts.'

'But it can never be our home again—the way it was once,' he said. 'At least under Monty's terms, we'd have had a piece of the action. It would have been better than nothing.'

'Not to me.' Courtney shook her head. 'Never to me. Oh, Rob, why didn't you come to me when it happened? I could have done something, perhaps. A bank loan or . . .'

A faint smile touched the corners of his mouth. 'I don't think they grant them for things like gambling debts. And I didn't want to involve you anyway. But now I've got to. I've come to you, Courtney, and there is something you can do to help. Take Blair Devereux away from the area and keep him away until the auction is over. Phone him and tell him you've changed your mind about Hylam Abbey.'

'Just like that?'

'Why not? He couldn't take his eyes off you last night. A call from you would flatter his ego. And you didn't turn him down flat, after all.'

'I suppose not,' she said dully. 'All right, Rob, I'll do as you ask.' She tried to summon a wry smile. 'I think I'd better take a long spoon.'

'What?' He gave her an uncomprehending look.

'Don't you remember Nanny's dire warnings when

we were small? She said a long spoon was what you needed to sup with the devil.'

'Now you're being over-dramatic,' he said impatiently. 'Just phone him, Courtney. It's not that much to ask.'

Not to him, Courtney thought, as reluctantly she lifted the receiver. But for her, compliance could have an untold cost.

CHAPTER THREE

COURTNEY waited. He'd said around ten-thirty, and she'd just heard the half hour strike from the parish church clock.

It had all been accomplished quite easily. She hoped she'd managed to make her tone sufficiently casual, in spite of the inevitable distortion of the telephone when she asked if last night's invitation was still open. Blair had said it was and although she had listened, ears straining, she hadn't heard a note of mockery.

But she hadn't got him to agree to let her come to the hotel to meet him, and this was a sore point. She didn't want Blair calling at the cottage, making comparisons. She didn't want Blair calling at the cottage, full stop.

Yet here she was, roaming the living room like a caged lioness, waiting for him to come.

She had dressed with a reasonable amount of care, prompted by Robin.

'Even if you don't want to spend the day with him, you can pretend, can't you?' he'd argued.

So she had put on the dark red wool suit with the gently bloused jacket, adding a high-necked sweater for warmth, because the brightness of the day was deceptive. In more ways than one, she thought bitterly as she applied a modicum of cosmetics, toning down the rather hectic flush on her cheekbones.

She'd been listening for the sound of the car, but the first thing she heard was the rapid tattoo of the door-knocker. He was all in black today, from the leather car coat to the close-fitting pants which gave emphasis to the lean muscled strength of his legs. His smile was slow, his eyes appreciative as they roamed over her.

He said, 'Hello, Courtney. Is the coffee ready?'

Before she could say anything, he had moved past

her into the living room, dropping his coat on to a chair.

'I thought we were going out,' she said flatly.

'We have the whole day.' He smiled again. 'You don't grudge me a cup of coffee before we set off, do you, Courtney?'

'Of course not.' She walked into the kitchen inwardly raging. 'Percolated or instant?' she called back.

'Instant, as you're in such a hurry to be off.' Blair appeared in the doorway, lounging against the jamb, watching as she set the kettle to boil, and put pottery mugs out on a tray. She didn't look at him, but she knew instinctively that he was looking round him, assimilating how small it all was, how cramped.

After a while, he said, 'I imagine you could cook a complete meal without moving your feet.'

Courtney would have liked to have hurled the boiling kettle at him.

Instead she said lightly, 'Saves wear and tear on shoe leather.'

'And that's a consideration?'

'Everything's a consideration in these hard times.' She poured boiling water into the mugs, stirring the mixture as if it required her total concentration. 'Milk? Sugar?'

'A little milk, thanks.' He accepted the mug she offered, then stood back with elaborate courtesy to allow her to precede him back into the living room. She took one of the chairs by the empty hearth. She usually perched on a corner of the sofa, but that might be interpreted as an invitation.

Rob wasn't a short man, but Blair Devereux would top him easily. He dwarfed the room, Courtney thought resentfully as she sipped the coffee she didn't want.

'Relax, Courtney,' he advised lazily. 'I thought it was only visitors who sat on the edge of their seats.'

She gave him a wintry smile. 'I'm afraid we'll miss the best of the weather. These fine days don't always last.'

'Let me worry about that,' he said. 'Where's Rob?'

'At work.' She leaned back against the cushions of

the chair, deliberately camouflaging her inward tensing at the lie.

'I'm amazed.' At her immediate startled look, Blair went on smoothly, 'I thought he would have still been recovering from his hangover.'

She shrugged. 'He must have a harder head than you imagine.'

'Clearly.' His voice was amused. 'It's not something I associate with him.'

She couldn't prevent the look of dislike she shot him. 'Perhaps you underestimate him.'

'I thought I'd learned not to underestimate any member of your family,' he said drily. 'How is your father, by the way?'

'He's a very sick man.'

'I'm sorry to hear it.' His voice held no particular expression, and Courtney's fingers tightened round her coffee mug.

He's a sick man, she thought and it's your fault—yours and your uncle's. He'd be fit and well today, but for you.

She said, 'He's in an excellent nursing home. We've been very fortunate.'

Blair's mouth twisted slightly. 'I'll take your word for that, Courtney. From poor little rich girl to poor little poor girl is a hell of a swoop.'

She said tautly, 'If you're tempted to feel sorry for me, please don't.'

'Don't worry,' he said. 'Pity isn't paramount among my emotions where you're concerned.'

Her teeth caught at the soft fullness of her inner lip. The conversation had taken too personal a turn altogether, and she had a day to face of it. She leaned down and put her empty mug in the hearth.

'Shall we be going?' She got to her feet, smoothing her hands down her skirt to remove the creases, and seeing with vexation that his glance followed the movement, tracing the outline of her body beneath the material.

She remembered Robin's words, *'He couldn't take*

his eyes off you all night', and she shivered inwardly.

She was on tenterhooks as they went out to the car in case Rob should suddenly put in an appearance, imagining them to be long gone. She almost sighed with relief as they left the village behind.

It wasn't a long way to the Abbey, but the route lay through winding lanes rather than a main road, and the Porsche purred along, unable to release its full power, and with any other companion Courtney would have been full of questions, full of interest about the car and its performance.

She sat, her hands folded in her lap in apparent tranquillity, but close observation would have revealed that the knuckles were white with strain. She had always supposed she had a root belief in natural justice, but Blair's affluence was enough to make her think again. He had an expensive car, good clothes and if last night's bill was anything to go by, money was no object with him.

For three years and more she had been counting the cost, while he flourished out of their ruin. Where was the justice in that? Anger was boiling in her, and frustration, but she had to mask it, and force herself to reply to his infrequent comments on the scenery and the weather with at least the appearance of civility.

There was a car park across the lane from the Abbey grounds, but the hut was unmanned during the winter months.

Courtney walked on ahead while Blair was locking the car. The breeze was light but chilly, and he wouldn't expect her to hang around, she told herself. It was very quiet, the only sound the cawing of rooks high in the tall trees. The gate squeaked as she pushed it open, and Blair coming up behind her took the weight of it from her, and pulled it to after them.

She thrust her gloved hands into the pockets of her jacket, keeping slightly ahead of him, edgy in case he tried to take her hand or her arm. She could play the part assigned to her only as long as she had to, which was about another hour by her estimation. But any attempt by him to touch her could precipitate a crisis she was by no means ready for.

Yet Blair didn't seem over-anxious to introduce any physical contact, she had to admit. He had brought a camera from the car, and his preoccupation seemed to be more with the focus and the light than it was with her.

The air was clear and clean, and she breathed it deeply, gratefully as they approached the ruins of the abbey. In the season when the tourists came, there were maps and booklets for sale, but Courtney didn't need them. She could walk among the tumbled stones and place the cloister, the dormitory, the refectory and the chapter house without thinking twice. The chapel stood slightly apart, its tall eastern wall with the empty windows probably the best preserved fragment of the entire abbey.

'So who were they?' Blair asked.

'Cistercians. Quite a small foundation, compared with the big Yorkshire abbeys like Jervaulx. The story goes that when Henry the Eighth's commissioners were going the rounds, dissolving the monasteries, the Abbot prayed that they might be too insignificant to attract the King's majestic notice, but his prayer wasn't answered. What little they had was taken, and the monks were turned out to wander the country.'

Blair said, ' *"Hark, hark, the dogs do bark, the beggars are coming to town."* That's the source of that particular nursery rhyme, as you probably know.'

'I didn't, actually,' Courtney admitted. 'But most of them seem to have pretty grisly roots. It was only after watching a play on television that I realised Ring of Roses referred back to the Plague.' She gave a little sigh as she looked around her. 'It seems so awful. I know a lot of monasteries were rich and corrupt, but this was such a small one, and the monks seem to have done a lot of good locally. Apparently it was years before any of the local people came to take the stone for building, because it was hoped one day the monks would return. But they didn't, of course.'

'And what happened to them?' Blair was watching her.

She shrugged. 'Made new lives for themselves, I suppose, or starved. There wasn't a great deal of choice in the good old days.' And there isn't now, she thought. The survivors go on, and the others go to the wall.

Blair looked slowly round, his hands resting lightly on his hips.

'And so it became a cheap source of building materials for the neighbouring landowners,' he commented. 'Hunters Court would have been the exception, of course.'

'I've never really thought about it,' she said uneasily, wondering why he had brought the house into the conversation.

'Why should you? They weren't Lincolns in those days.'

'No,' she said. 'The—the Lincolns came into the property later around the time of William and Mary.'

'Their predecessors being Catholics,' he said. 'Who fled to France with James the Second.'

She said coolly, 'History isn't one of my passions, I'm afraid.'

'I'd have thought ordinary curiosity would have made you want to know something about the men and women who built the house in which you spent your formative years . . .'

Courtney shrugged. 'There's very little of the original building left,' she said shortly. 'There were a lot of alterations and additions over a great many years.'

'Naturally,' he said. 'It's in the nature of generations to leave some mark for posterity. Hunters Court has fared neither better nor worse than most old houses in this respect.'

And what's posterity going to think of this generation's efforts? Courtney wondered painfully. Neon lights and discotheques.

Blair said abruptly, 'Is something wrong?'

She recovered with a start. 'No—should there be?'

He was watching her, frowning a little. 'I thought you might have seen the Abbot's ghost.'

Courtney forced a smile. 'Is there one? I've never heard of it.'

'I wouldn't know,' he said coolly. 'You're the expert on this place, and for someone who doesn't care for history, you know quite a lot.'

'Perhaps,' she said. 'But it isn't the history I care for. It's the atmosphere. Even on a summer day with hordes of people milling around, it seems to retain an essential tranquillity—oh, I can't explain.'

'You seem to be making a fair job of it,' he said rather drily. 'Go on—please.'

She paused. 'Well, I don't think there are ghosts as such, but I do think the Cistercian spirit still lingers—the austerity, the liking for seclusion.' She forced a smile. 'It sounds ridiculous.'

'No, it doesn't,' he said. 'Why mock something you obviously feel sincerely?'

Because it was something I didn't want—didn't intend you to see, she thought.

He went on 'Did you ever feel any Jesuit spirit hanging round Hunters Court?'

'What do you mean?'

He lifted one shoulder. 'I presume the priest's hole still exists—or did it vanish with the alterations and additions you mentioned?'

'I haven't the slightest idea.' And it was true. She'd never heard anyone mention such a thing. 'Do you mean—a secret passage?'

'Nothing as elaborate as that,' said Blair. 'Probably a hidden cupboard big enough to hide a chalice and vestments, and a man at a pinch, although it would have been terribly cramped. But you've never heard of it—never seen it?'

'Never.' She drew a breath. 'I'm sure you must be mistaken.'

'I don't think so. At one time I made quite a study of the house's history, particularly its earliest days. Someone—your grandfather I think—had sent a load of documents, journals, old account books, all kind of things, to the County archives. I saw them there. There was a receipt among them for a local carpenter for some unknown task to do with a "place of safe-keeping". And I've read in various local history books that in Queen Elizabeth's time it was said that priests were being "harboured" at Hunters Court.'

'I expect there would have been—if the people were Catholics,' Courtney said. 'But it doesn't prove anything. I imagine there were similar rumours about any family with Catholic leanings. But if there was a priest's hole at Hunters Court, then we would have known about it.' She laughed. 'Rob and I would have bragged about it to everyone. It's far more of a talking point than a lake and a rose garden.'

He said, 'Perhaps your ancestors found it and decided to block it up.'

It was the obvious answer, she thought, reviewing in her mind the rather stolid features of the family portraits of the period. They wouldn't have thought a priest's hole was romantic, those staunch supporters of William of Orange. They would have found it an embarrassment. Courtney was slightly embarrassed herself. It seemed wrong that Blair should have this knowledge, this inside information, when she'd been totally unaware that such a thing might have existed.

She bitterly resented the thought of him poring for hours over old papers and yellowing ink, discovering things about Hunters Court and the Lincolns that she would never know.

Damn him, she thought angrily. Why couldn't he mind his own business?

While he was taking some photographs, Courtney stole a surreptitious glance at her watch, and saw to her satisfaction that it was almost midday. She sat on a stone and lifted her face to the sun, counting away the minutes in her mind.

She hadn't had time to think about what Robin had told her of his indebtedness to Monty Pallister, but now she began to consider his position with growing concern. She understood now why he had been so ready to fall in with Monty's plans, and apparently give them his support, although she could not condone it.

He'd behaved like an utter fool, she told herself roundly, but did he realise it fully? He'd asked for her help, but she hadn't sensed much remorse or self-reproach in his attitude. Oh, he'd been sorry enough for himself, but the doubtful morality of his actions had apparently escaped him.

And now it seemed that Monty Pallister's hold on Robin was going to continue for the foreseeable future. He isn't just going to employ him, Courtney thought unhappily, he's going to own him, and Rob will have to dance to whatever tune he chooses to play.

All her old suspicions and fears about Pallister's motives and methods had been revived by Robin's confession. He was capable of anything, it seemed, and she had little confidence that Robin would be able to make a stand against his demands. He was weak, and she'd always known it, so she had to be strong for them both.

I'll get some extra work, she thought, typing to do at home in the evenings. I'll advertise. I'll use the money to pay Monty Pallister back, so that Rob can be free eventually, no matter how long it takes.

But in her heart, she knew that the sooner would be the better. No one as easily led as Robin should be exposed to anyone as dubious as Monty Pallister for too long, or it could lead to disaster.

She sighed. Thank heaven her father had no idea what was happening! News of this kind could have the most serious effect on his condition. Courtney was always careful to present a smiling tranquil exterior when she visited him, no matter how troubled or insecure she might be feeling, and it was often a strain. Often she had longed to put her head down on his lap and sob away all her fears and uncertainties as she'd done when she was a child, but it was impossible. The doctor had been blunt. Mr Lincoln must not be worried or overly excited, he had warned, or he could not answer for the possible consequences.

She shivered suddenly, conscious as never before of her vulnerability and isolation.

Above her Blair's voice said with sudden brusqueness, 'You're cold. Let's get out of here and go and have lunch.'

He was putting out a hand to help her to her feet, but the thought of his touching her made her feel cold and sick and she lifted herself off her seat with a rush, almost stumbling in her haste to put herself out of his reach.

The realisation of everything that he and his family had done to her and hers struck at her.

She said in a strangled voice, 'No, I don't want lunch. I want to go home.'

Blair was frowning, and the little scar on his cheek seemed to throb slightly. 'What's the matter? Are you ill?'

'No.' She could have eased her way out of the situation with a lie, but it no longer mattered what he thought, she told herself. 'I've just had enough, that's all.'

'Is it indeed?' He sent her a narrow-eyed look. 'When we spoke on the phone earlier, I got the impression we were going to spend the day together.'

'Then you were mistaken,' she said. 'I agreed to come here with you because it's one of my favourite places, and I thought not even your company could poison it for me, but I was wrong.'

There was a brief taut silence, then he said slowly, 'While we're speaking so frankly, may I know what prompted you to accept my invitation—feeling as you do?'

'I had my reasons,' she said shortly. 'If you're not prepared to drive me home, there's a phone box by the main gates, and I can call a taxi.'

'I'm sure you'd prefer me to leave you stranded,' he drawled. 'It would be one more item on the list of wrongs you're compiling against me, wouldn't it, Courtney? I imagined the intervening years might have taught you a little sense, but I see I was wrong.'

She said hotly, 'If that's the case, then I'm surprised you made the invitation to me in the first place!'

He smiled unpleasantly. 'Oh, but I too had my reasons, Courtney. Or did you think I'd been so overwhelmed by your undoubted charms I couldn't wait to get you alone?'

'Your motives don't interest me in the slightest,' she snapped, but she was aware of a slight flush rising in her cheeks. 'May we go now, please?'

'By all means,' he agreed coolly.

She walked ahead of him to the car park, thankful that he was apparently content to leave her alone. She supposed it had been Robin who had prompted this present situation, although Blair had been keen enough to ask her to go out with him at their first encounter in the grounds at Hunters Court.

Not that it mattered, she assured herself. All that counted was that she would, she hoped, never have to see him again. Certainly there would be no further invitations forthcoming after this morning's fiasco.

The drive back to the village was accomplished in the same rather brooding silence, and in spite of herself Courtney could feel tension rising within her. She tried to tell herself that it was concern to find out how Rob had fared at the auction, but in her heart she knew it wasn't as simple as that.

She wished she hadn't allowed her deep-seated bitterness to take command. It would have been wiser to have accepted Blair's suggestion that they should have lunch, and made her excuses gracefully when the meal was over. Instead she had gone out of her way to antagonise him, even though every instinct suggested he was a bad man to cross.

It would have been more sensible to have followed Rob's lead, and pretended that the past no longer mattered, and that time had healed all wounds.

But I can't, she thought almost desperately. There's too much between us.

Each time he looked in the mirror to shave, he must

see the mark she had left on him and remember that if
her aim had been better, the blow could have been
deadly.

And she was marked too, she realised, although her
scars were hidden. She had never told anyone about
those few taut minutes in the rose garden when Blair's
lips and arms had shown her the promise of passion.
She had tried too often to wipe them from her mind,
pretend it had never happened, but it was impossible.
And seeing him again had revived every memory only
too vividly, arousing feelings of anger and disgust deep
inside her.

As the car drew up outside the cottage, she said
stiltedly, 'Well, thank you for—a pleasant outing.'

He gave a brief unamused laugh. 'Isn't it a little late
to think about the social graces, Courtney? You put on
quite an act earlier. Your reasons for coming out with
me must certainly have been compelling ones.'

'They certainly were,' she agreed sweetly.

'Then let's hope they're good enough to survive this,'
he said gently. His hands reached for her, gripping her
shoulders, dragging her towards him, and even as her
lips parted in horrified protest, his mouth took
possession of hers with devastating force.

She moaned in her throat as the ruthless, draining
kiss went on and on. He had pulled her half out of her
seat, so she was totally off balance, and now he had one
arm round her body, and the other hand clamped at the
back of her head like a vice. She pushed feebly against
his chest in an enforcedly tacit rejection, but the
warmth of his body was like an electric current, sending
a tingling sensation through the palms of her hands.

Deep inside she felt a surge of unwilling, almost
bewildered feeling. What was happening to her? Blair
was her enemy: that was the rock she must cling to
before she began to drown in unaccustomed sensation.
No one had ever kissed her like this before. Certainly
Clive had never explored her mouth, tasting its
sweetness with such heart-stopping intimacy, as Blair
was doing, while his hand relaxed the first cruelty of its

grip to move smoothly and rhythmically at the base of her spine.

When at last he lifted his mouth from hers, her head would have fallen back helplessly if his other hand hadn't still been there, supporting her, his fingers twined in the long dark strands of her hair. She could hardly breathe, she was incapable of speech. All she could do was stare helplessly up into his face, searching—for what?

He said, 'Are you going to invite me into the cottage, Courtney? I can't make love to you here.'

Her body began to tremble as she realised how disastrously easy it would be to accede to his suggestion. It wouldn't even need words. All she would have to do was touch him—his face, or perhaps the curve of his shoulder, or offer him her mouth again, and they would be lovers in every sense of the word.

She shrank into her seat as the enormity of what she was thinking came home to her. And every moment she remained silent was an act of betrayal both to herself, and of her family.

She said hoarsely, 'No.'

He smiled faintly, 'I'm glad you agree.'

'I don't agree,' she blazed, self-contempt igniting her anger. 'How dare you even imagine . . .' Words failed her, and she turned away, fumbling for the door catch.

'Imagination has nothing to do with it,' he said. 'On the contrary, I'm being practical in the extreme. You're not a child any more, Courtney. You know where kissing leads. I want to touch you—and touch you without your clothes. The open street in broad daylight is hardly an appropriate place.'

She said thickly, 'You're disgusting!'

'And you're a hypocrite,' he returned. 'You want exactly what I want, so why pretend?'

'You've got an ego!' she snapped, and managed an unsteady laugh. 'If this is a sample of your technique, Blair, I'm not impressed. Do all your ladies fall into your arms so readily?'

'No,' he said. 'But they don't regard playing hard to

get as a particular virtue either.'

'And you think that's what I'm doing? You conceited swine!'

'I'm a realist.' His tone hardened. 'Why don't you try being one too?'

'Your kind of realism doesn't appeal to me.' Courtney shook her head, thankful that her breathing was steadying at last, and that the awful tremulous weakness which had invaded her body was beginning to retreat. 'Reaching out and taking whatever you want, regardless of whether it belongs to you or not, may be one of your family traits. It certainly isn't one of mine.'

She'd expected anger in return, but there was only faint mockery in his eyes as he watched her.

'And who do you reckon to belong to, Courtney?' he asked softly. 'Not, I trust, your ardent swain of last night?'

A dull flush heated her face. 'Clive at least has a sense of decency . . .'

'Which I lack,' he supplied as she hesitated. 'I suppose in a moment you'll be telling me I'm not fit to clean his shoes, or some other cliché. You're incredible, Courtney. I thought you might have grown up in the intervening years since we last met, but I see I was wrong.'

'Oh, I see.' she said, poisonously sweet. 'This whole little interlude was a kindly thought on your part to assist me to greater maturity. If I'd realised, I'd had been more grateful.'

'I doubt it.' His mouth twisted slightly. 'And I don't want your gratitude.'

'What do you want?' The question was out before she could stop herself.

He hesitated. 'Would you believe—a little honesty.'

Courtney shrugged. 'Are you sure you'd recognise it?'

'Try me,' he invited silkily.

'With pleasure.' She drew a breath. 'I hate you, Blair Devereux. I always have, and I always will, and nothing that you've said or done today has altered that, except to make me despise you as well. I'd hoped with all my heart that I'd never have to see you again. Is that honest enough for you?'

'It will do,' he said coolly. He leaned across her, his arm brushing her body as he freed the recalcitrant door catch. 'Off you go, then, darling. I hope the worthy Clive lives up to your expectations—it would be terrible if your hopes were to be blighted a second time.'

She got out of the car and stood for a moment looking at him, wanting to find something which would pierce his armour and hurt him.

'I don't need your concern,' she said at last. 'I don't know why you came back here, Blair, because no one wants you. Please go away, and this time stay away.'

There wasn't a sign of resentment in his face, or his relaxed body. He was even smiling a little.

'You're going to be disappointed again, Courtney. I've no intention of leaving.' The smile widened cruelly. 'In fact, I've bought a house here. Did I forget to mention it?'

He reached across and removed the handle of the car door from her suddenly slackened grasp, slamming it shut. He lifted one hand in a mocking salute, then the engine burst into life, and he drove off, leaving her standing there looking after him, her face stricken.

The cottage was empty. She had called Robin's name until she was hoarse, but there was no response. She forced herself to think calmly and rationally, to do ordinary everyday things like washing up the coffee mugs they had used, and preparing vegetables for the evening meal. An hour dragged by and she felt like screaming. Where was Robin?

Not that there was anything ominous in his continued absence, she quickly reassured herself. He could well be celebrating. Or perhaps Monty Pallister had summoned him to give him instructions of some kind, now that Hunters Court was his. Because the house did belong to him, she told herself vigorously, and she would have to come to terms with it. Any other possibility was—unthinkable.

The more she thought about, the more she was inclined to discount Blair's parting shot. He couldn't be so thick-skinned as to imagine he could simply walk back into the locality and be accepted when everyone knew what his uncle had done. No, he'd simply been trying to upset her. That was the only feasible explanation. Besides, you couldn't buy a house just like that. He hadn't been in the area long enough to look around him, or he would have been seen and word would have got about.

Unless he was planning to buy at an auction, an unwanted voice prodded in her mind. Courtney threw down the newspaper crossword she'd been staring at unseeingly, and snatched up her jerkin and her car keys. She couldn't sit around here waiting and wondering all day. She would drive over to Wolverton and visit her father.

The sun had given up the struggle altogether she realised as she drove the twenty-odd miles which separated the village from the market town where the nursing home was situated. Dull grey clouds had gathered, and there was a hint of icy rain in the air. Winter was by no means over, Courtney thought with a sigh.

The nursing home itself was a large Edwardian house standing in its own grounds on the outskirts of the town. Supported by a charitable trust which operated a number of similar establishments in other parts of the country, it offered a high standard of care. No matter how much Rob might resent its charitable aspect, they could never themselves afford the fees that other private homes asked.

Day Sister, who answered the door, looked surprised. 'Why, Miss Lincoln! This isn't your usual day.'

'No.' Courtney stripped off her driving gloves, pushing them into her bag. 'I had some time off from work, that's all.' She looked at Sister, her brows drawing together. 'Daddy—he isn't worse, is he?'

'On the contrary,' Sister said briskly. 'He seems to be making real progress. The therapist was with him earlier, and she's delighted with him. I daresay she would be glad to have a word with you.'

Miss Watson, the therapist, was a fresh-faced woman in her thirties with calm eyes and a pleasant smile. As Courtney rose from her seat in the waiting room to greet her, she wasted little time in coming to the point.

'I think you'll see a considerable change in him. I can't really understand or explain it myself. For a long time, as you know, he didn't seem prepared to try at all. Now he does all I ask and more.' Her eyes twinkled. 'I don't know what your brother said to him on his last visit, but it seems to have made all the difference.'

Courtney returned the smile rather rigidly. 'Then that's all that matters,' she said. She knew exactly what Rob had said, and it disturbed her that it should have had such an overwhelming effect on her father.

'I won't pretend that your father won't always be an invalid,' Miss Watson went on, 'But he's regaining more of his speech every day, and in time he may be able to walk—with mechanical aids of some kind. We can discuss that more fully at some future visit.' She gave Courtney a kindly look. 'Now I'm sure you want to see him and witness some of this miracle for yourself.'

The change in James Lincoln was visible even to Courtney. His eyes were bright, and his face had begun to lose the shrunken look it had worn for so long. He smiled as Courtney came into the room. 'Darling,' he said with something of an effort, and held out his hand.

Courtney sank down on the chair beside the bed, and kissed him.

'You look wonderful,' she told him steadily, concealing her inner disquiet. If he could be so easily built up by Robin's plans for Hunters Court, what effect might there be if something had—gone wrong? She didn't want to formulate her fears any more directly than that.

'Feel—wonderful,' he said. 'How's—Rob?'

In other words, how is the purchase of the house proceeding? Courtney thought worriedly.

'Fine,' she said casually. 'He's very busy these days, but I'm sure he'll be over to see you soon.'

'Yes.' There was an expression of triumphant satisfaction in James Lincoln's eyes as he leaned back against the pillows. It was obvious that he expected Robin to have good news when he came. Courtney guessed he had no idea that the auction had been held that very day, and Hunters Court's fate decided, or he would have been agitated.

'You know—all about it?' His eyes were searching her face.

'Yes.' Courtney hesitated. 'Daddy, don't you mind?'

The slight movement of the head was in the negative. 'Beggars,' he said slowly and carefully, 'can't be choosers.' For a moment the drawn look was back as if he was comparing the past with the present situation and finding the contrast painful, and her heart bled for him.

'Oh, Dad!' She lifted his hand and put it against her cheek. All her life she had been cherished. She had been able to take her slightest problem to him since early childhood, and he had always listened, never indicating by the smallest word or slightest gesture that he might find any of them ridiculous and trivial, although frequently they'd been both. Now she was oppressed by all kinds of troubles, and she couldn't say a word.

Never again could she have the sheer luxury of unburdening her miseries on to her father's shoulders, and yet she had never needed to more than she did at this moment. She had to be the strong one, the protector now, and the responsibility of it weighed her down. She couldn't even rely on Rob. She never had been able to, she realised with resignation.

And if her brother had met not with triumph but disaster at the auction, she had little doubt who would have to break the news to her father as gently as she could.

Oh, damn Rob! she thought savagely. Why couldn't he have kept his mouth shut until everything was signed and settled?

And if the deal with Monty Pallister had gone irretrievably sour, what other bad news might she have to pass on to James Lincoln? She shuddered inwardly as she remembered the fear in Rob's eyes. What a mess everything was, and to top it all, there was Blair Devereux insulting her, pawing her, forcing her to accept his disgusting kisses.

She swallowed. Thank goodness that was one thing that her father need never know about, whatever else happened.

She was thankful too that he would never know how dangerously, disastrously close she had come to surrender. However briefly, there had been moments when she had wanted Blair's kisses, and more. She had wanted to feel his body against hers, to feel his hands touching her in all the ways there were.

It was degrading, but she had to face it. He had made her want him in those few delirious minutes. He had made her experience feelings, sensations she had never been aware of before. She had once read that physical passion was the great betrayer of humanity. Now she understood and believed it.

The chemistry between two bodies was cruel and arbitrary, and no respecter of justice or reason.

But she was warned now, and could guard against her own untutored senses. All she need do if Blair ever got close enough again to make love to her was remember her father, struck down in the prime of his life.

'An invalid,' Miss Watson said. Nothing could ever change that. James Lincoln would never again be the strong, vital, successful man that he had once been. And for that Blair Devereux was to blame, she thought bitterly. That terrible scene after his uncle's arrest when he had forced his way into Hunters Court, shouting, storming, accusing, had been the final straw.

Just for a while she had been seduced with kisses into forgetting. But it wouldn't happen again.

'Never again,' said a small fierce voice, deep within her, and her slender hands clenched suddenly into fists to acknowledge and underline the silent vow.

CHAPTER FOUR

MONTY PALLISTER's Jaguar was parked aggressively in front of the cottage when Courtney returned that evening, and she groaned as she drove her car round to the rear yard and put it away. She lifted the latch on the back door and let herself into the kitchen, wincing as the sound of loud angry voices assaulted her ears.

The air in the living room was thick with cigar smoke, and Courtney could not control an angry grimace as she stood in the doorway. This was her home, after all, and she resented having it polluted by cigars and whisky fumes, and above all by the violence she sensed in the room.

She looked for Robin at once, and found him sitting on the sofa, his face pale and miserable. So—the final confirmation that the worst had happened, she thought resignedly as she glanced round to see who else was there.

Monty Pallister, naturally, dominated the room from the rug in front of the hearth. The genial veneer had been stripped away, and the plump shiny face, reddened by anger as well as the warmth of the room, looked crude and brutal. The two men with him were vaguely familiar. One of them was an architect, and the other one an accountant, Courtney thought.

Pallister had seen her. He swung round to face her, his bushy brows drawing together. 'So you're back.'

Courtney lifted her chin. 'I live here. May I ask what you're doing here?'

Robin said her name in an unhappy undertone, but she ignored him.

'Don't get on your high horse with me,' Pallister sneered. 'Do you know what this bloody fool of a brother of yours has done?' His voice rose angrily, veins

71

standing out on his forehead. He's lost me Hunters Court, that's what!'

'So I've gathered,' Courtney said drily. 'Is this a post-mortem?'

Her cool tone made Monty Pallister pause, even though his glare did not diminish. Courtney walked across the room and put a hand on Robin's shoulder.

'Hello, love,' she said quietly. 'Would you like some coffee?'

He shook his head. 'Nothing, thanks,' he returned in a low voice. 'Courtney—I . . .'

'Hush!' Her fingers pressed his shoulder. She looked at Monty Pallister. 'I think we've all had a trying day. Perhaps you'll leave my home now.'

'I'm damned if I will!' Pallister's chin jutted. 'Not until this idiot's explained what the hell he's been playing at—with my money. I should have known better than to use a bloody amateur!'

'Yes, probably you should,' Courtney agreed. 'Now will you go, please?'

'Not without my money.' There was a dangerous glitter in the pale eyes as they looked at her. 'Your thief of a brother was well paid to do a job for me, and he hasn't done it. Oh, he could buy the house,' he added contemptuously. 'He knew everyone, he could oil the wheels, he could get it cheap. And I believed him!'

'That was your mistake.' Courtney refused to be intimidated. 'A man of your business acumen should have known better than to employ an—inexperienced boy.' She felt Robin flinch as she spoke.

'He's not such a boy.' The sneering tone was back. 'He wasn't a boy when he started gambling in one of my clubs, losing money he didn't have. He wasn't a boy when we finalised our deal. Oh, he was a big man then.'

'And just what do you hope to achieve by coming here bullying him?' Courtney demanded indignantly.

Pallister hauled a handkerchief out of his pocket and mopped his face with it. 'I want that house,' he said. 'And your brother's going to get it for me, if he knows what's good for him. Come on, you two.' He jerked his head at his silent companions. 'We'll leave him to think about it.' His gaze returned to Courtney. He said in a flat tone, 'I'll be back tomorrow.'

She almost gasped with relief when the door closed behind them. She turned to Robin, sinking down on to the sofa beside him.

'What happened?' she urged gently.

He shook his head. 'He's right, Courtney,' he said wearily. 'I was a bloody fool. I didn't know what I was doing. I thought the house was mine, and at a good price too. I was—cock-a-hoop. There was no one else left in the bidding. I heard Frank Mottram mention another figure, and I thought he was just trying to force the price up again. I didn't realise . . .' His voice tailed away. 'I didn't realise he was acting for someone—I didn't know they could do that. I—I stopped bidding—and I lost.'

Courtney heard him out, dismay knotted tightly in her stomach.

She said, 'Who was Frank Mottram acting for? Do you know?'

'Oh, yes.' Rob nodded dully. 'I know.' He drew a deep breath, and his voice thickened. 'It was Blair—Blair Devereux.'

The possibility had haunted her all afternoon, and she had comforted herself with the fact that he had missed the auction. Like Robin, it had never occurred to her that he didn't actually need to be present.

What fools he'd made of them both, she thought, staring sightlessly in front of her. He'd played them along all the time, and they'd swallowed the bait almost eagerly. How amused he must have been, she thought, writhing inwardly, when she had telephoned him that morning. He must have been laughing silently at her all the time they were at the Abbey, knowing the effort it was costing her to be civil, and totally unsurprised at her change of attitude when at last she'd thought herself safe.

She said tonelessly, 'You're sure? There couldn't possibly be—a mistake?'

'Only the one I made,' Robin said bitterly. 'What a mess I've made of everything! What am I going to do?'

'There isn't a great deal you can do.' She tried to speak gently. Poor Rob, always so cocksure, so resentful of advice or criticism. There was a silence, then she said, 'I—I saw Daddy today. Telling him is going to be the worst thing.'

Robin shook his head. 'Not the worst thing,' he said flatly. He swallowed. 'I've got to get the house for Monty—either that or repay him the money he advanced me. I've got to.'

Courtney stared at him, all her unease revived by the note of rising panic in his voice.

'There's no way you'll get the house,' she said after a moment's pause. 'As for the money—well, you'll have to pay it back. He'll have to give you time.'

Robin shook his head. 'No time,' he said in a strangled voice. 'Before you came in—before the other two arrived—he was here. I've never seen him like that. I'd rung him you see and told him what had happened and he told me to wait here for him. And I did.'

'It was natural he should be in a temper,' she pointed out. 'You've cost him a great deal of inconvenience, after all, and . . .'

'No, listen—listen. He came in alone. He wasn't as you saw him—angry and swearing. He was very quiet. He said I'd made the whole operation look ridiculous, that I'd made him look a fool. He said, "I didn't pay you for that. I paid you for results, and you either get me that house or I call in my loan at the end of the week."'

'But that's impossible,' Courtney protested. 'You can't possibly find a sum like that in such a short . . .'

'I know.' Robin raised tortured eyes to her face. 'I tried to say this—and he laughed. He said, "The house—or the money, friend, or you'll be a cripple like your father. I have associates who don't mess about.'

The words fell about her like stones. Her mouth went dry and she moistened her lips swiftly with the tip of her tongue, while she searched for something to say.

There was no point in asking Robin if he was sure that was what had been said, or even suggesting that Pallister's threat was an empty one. This was what she had always sensed, coiled in the man, like a snake under a rock. The successful businessman with his expensive car and tailored suits was only a cloak for the thug.

Robin said again, 'What am I going to do?'

'I don't know,' Courtney admitted tiredly. She squared her shoulders, getting up from the sofa. 'I'll make us something to eat.'

'I'm not hungry.'

'Do you think I am?' Her smile was a parody of itself. 'But we need to think, and fasting makes you lightheaded, I understand.'

The vegetables she had prepared earlier seemed to belong to another lifetime. She cooked them while she grilled chops she'd taken from the small fridge.

Robin didn't move while she laid the table, but when she brought in the food, he came to the table and went through the motions of eating. Afterwards she made strong coffee, and added one of the sleeping tablets she took occasionally to Robin's cup. He was beginning to yawn before the washing up was finished.

Courtney needed a sleeping pill herself, but she didn't take one. Instead she lay awake, letting all the events of that disastrous day parade endlessly through her mind. But no matter how much her brain twisted and turned, in the end every avenue of thought led back only to Blair.

She squeezed her eyelids together, trying to blot the image of him out, but it didn't work. Wincing, she knew he was too firmly implanted, altogether too three-dimensional. All too clearly she could see him, his scarred cheek, and the little devils dancing in his hazel eyes. She could remember other things too—the scent of his skin which she'd been forced to breathe, the taste of his mouth on hers. She lifted her clenched fist to her mouth and suppressed a little moan.

He'd come back for revenge: she knew that now. He wanted their ruin completed. It wasn't enough for him that they'd lost their home, and their money, and that her father was a sick man. He wanted more, and he'd achieved it.

We were duly warned, she acknowledged to the darkness. That mention of Monty Pallister should have told us that he knew exactly what Rob was up to. Only we didn't want to believe it . . .

Now he'd taken the house for himself, and only a few hours earlier he might have taken her too, in this very bed. That, and the certain knowledge that he had destroyed Robin, because if he knew Monty Pallister at all then he knew the kind of man he was dealing with, might have satisfied him.

None of Pallister's revolting threats and bullying frightened her as much as the thought of Blair Devereux, and the waiting game he'd played all this time.

She asked herself, as Robin had done, 'What am I going to do?'

She still had no answer when morning came. Robin was still fast asleep, and she made no attempt to wake him up. On most Saturday mornings she did housework, and this one would be no exception. It was still raining, but slightly milder, and she opened the downstairs windows as she worked to rid the place of the last vestige of cigar-smoke. She vacuumed and dusted and polished until the cottage was shining again, and felt like the home she had made.

She filled the log basket, and had just lit the fire and was standing up, dusting her hands on her jean-clad thighs, when she realised that Monty Pallister was in the room, watching her.

She said icily, 'I prefer visitors to wait until they're invited in.'

'I'm hardly a visitor, dear,' he said. 'More a friend of the family,' He smiled.

Courtney realised that the good-humoured façade was back in place today.

'That's hardly the description I'd use,' she said acidly.

The round pale face beamed at her. 'Come now, dear, don't bear a grudge. Your young brother made me very angry yesterday, I admit, and perhaps I went a little far with him, but I think I can be excused. Oh yes.'

He sat down on the sofa, the pale eyes fixed on her.

'This man who bought Hunters Court,' he said. 'Apparently you know him.'

'Yes.' Judiciously Courtney added another log to the fire.

'What sort of man is he? I mean, is he open to reason?'

In other words, can he be bought like Robin, she thought. She shrugged. 'He's staying at the pub. Why don't you ask him?'

'He's not there, dear, or I might have done. He didn't stay there last night.' He took out a cigar case. 'Did he give you any hint yesterday where he was going? I understand you were with him.'

'None at all,' she said calmly. 'Rob is still asleep, but I suppose I can wake him up if you want to talk to him.'

'I've come to talk to you.' Pallister lit the cigar with care, and studied her with narrowed eyes through the blue smoke. 'I blame myself for trusting young Robin. I should have seen that you were the man of the family.'

'Thank you,' Courtney said with irony.

The fleshy lips stretched in a smile. 'You haven't always been as—friendly to me as you might have been, Courtney. But I'm a forgiving man, or I could be.'

The use of her Christian name put her on her guard. Before it had always been 'Miss Lincoln' interspersed with the hated 'dear'. Now there was an implication of a new familiarity which worried her.

He went on, 'Really, you see, your young brother needs to be taught a lesson. That's the way some of my friends feel about it—the ones that stand to lose money because of his carelessness. But it doesn't have to happen. It rather depends on you.'

After a pause, she said, 'I don't quite see how. If you imagine that Blair Devereux would be willing to sell me the house on your behalf, then you're wrong.'

'Oh, he'll sell me the house,' he said confidently, 'if I offer him enough money. He's not working for anyone. I've had enquiries made. He just wants it as a place to live in, and there are plenty of other properties on the market which would do as well for him. I'll make it worth his while to find one of them.' He paused for a moment. 'But that doesn't alter the fact that Robin let us all down badly. Some of my associates will feel—do feel that an example should be made, just so that no one else on our payroll is tempted to do less than his best.'

Courtney felt sick.

'On the other hand,' Monty Pallister said slowly, 'I could persuade them to overlook his mistake—this time.' He put the cigar down and got to his feet.

'Then I hope you will.' Courtney tried to speak calmly, as if her skin had not started to crawl.

He tutted as he came towards her. 'Just like that? You'll have to do better than that, dear, if you want me to help you get your brother off the hook. You'll have to make up for the times when you haven't been— friendly.'

'I'll see you in hell first,' Courtney said in a low voice.

He laughed, the pale eyes fixing greedily on her mouth. 'Come on, dear, you're more of a realist than that. You're a good-looking girl. You know what it's all about.'

Before she could resist, he had enveloped her in a suffocating embrace, his mouth pressing wetly on hers in a shocking travesty of a kiss, while one hand fumbled under her sweater to reach her breast.

For a few seconds Courtney was too horrified even to struggle, then she began to fight wildly, striking at him, raking at the plump moist flesh with her nails.

He swore and let her go, his hand going up to his

scratches to see if he was bleeding.

'Bitch,' he said hoarsely.

Blair Devereux said, 'The lady doesn't seem to relish your advances.'

Courtney stood, breasts heaving, fighting to draw breath into her lungs.

'What the hell——' Monty Pallister began aggressively.

'The front door was open,' Blair explained, 'so I walked straight in. But perhaps I misread the situation. Perhaps I'm intruding. Am I, Courtney?'

She shook her head in silence.

Monty Pallister was recovering swiftly, finding his smile. 'Miss Lincoln and I were discussing some business.'

'From what I saw, the discussion was a little one-sided,' Blair said drily. 'The door is still open. I recommend you use it, unless you'd prefer to be thrown out.'

Watching almost detachedly, Courtney saw the red angry flush rise in Pallister's face, and the venom in the pale eyes. She turned her head away, and then the swift slam of the front door told her he had gone.

She began to tremble. The reek of his aftershave seemed to be all around her, in her hair, on her clothes.

Courtney said in a muffled voice, 'I think I'm going to be sick.'

He moved swiftly, manoeuvring her effortlessly into the kitchen and over to the sink before the worst happened. When the paroxysm had passed, she wanted to cry with shock and humiliation. It was bad enough being sick in front of someone, but when that someone was Blair Devereux, it became a hundred times worse. He was the last person she'd want to see her in such a shameful state of weakness.

He helped her back into the living room and settled her on the sofa, with a cool damp cloth across her forehead.

She said, not looking at him, 'May I have a glass of water?'

'Brandy might be better, if there is any.'

When she shook her head, he fetched the water, and stood looking down at her while she sipped.

He said abruptly, 'You're not very fortunate in your suitors, Courtney. A boy and a rogue—not even a pleasant one.'

'Please don't concern yourself.' She was beginning to regain her self-control. 'What are you doing here anyway?'

'Apparently rescuing you from a fate worse than death,' he said sardonically.

'Well, it wasn't necessary,' she snapped.

'I'm sorry.' He didn't sound in the least repentant. 'Do you want me to call him back?'

Courtney drank some more water in silence. Then she said, 'Have you come here to gloat?'

'Should I?'

She lifted one shoulder. 'Why did you buy Hunters Court.'

'Because I've always wanted it. My life has changed sufficiently over the past three years to enable me to buy the things I want.'

She said bitterly, 'As simple as that. You knew of course that Rob was acting for Monty Pallister and his—friends at the auction?'

'Yes, I knew.' His voice was harsh. 'But what I still don't know is why? The man is scum, and his so-called developments match him in every way. Couldn't your brother see that, or was he too blinded by his money to notice?'

'You'll soon be able to answer that yourself,' Courtney said wearily. 'I understand he's about to make you an offer you can't refuse.'

The firm lips smiled grimly. 'I doubt it.'

'You mean because of what happened just now?' Courtney shook her head. 'He won't allow a little confrontation like that to stand in the way of business.'

'You misunderstand me,' Blair said drily. 'No offer by Mr Pallister or any of his sort could ever be in any way acceptable to me.'

Courtney swung her legs to the floor, pulling the cloth from her forehead. He'd used his handkerchief, she noticed almost absently. Pure linen, expensive with a monogram in the corner.

'Really?' She lifted her chin. 'I'd have thought you would have had a lot in common.'

There was a short dead silence, then he said quietly, 'And what am I supposed to infer from that remark?'

That your uncle stole from us, ruined us, and you're now a rich man, she thought, but she dared not utter the words aloud.

She shook her head. 'It doesn't matter.' She hesitated, then said stiffly, 'Thank you for coming to my assistance just now. There's no need for you to stay any longer.'

'Graciously spoken.' Blair sounded faintly amused. 'But I didn't come here to protect you from Pallister's clumsy attentions. I came to talk to you—and to Robin,' he added.

Courtney stared down at the worn carpet. 'There's nothing you have to say that either of us could want to hear. Please go and leave us alone.'

There was the sound of movement upstairs, footsteps, and then the door which closed off the stairway from the living room opened and Robin came in, dressed with ruffled hair.

He was yawning as he said, 'It's late! Is there any coffee ...' His voice tailed away as he caught sight of Blair, then his eyes went swiftly to Courtney. He demanded, 'What the hell have you been doing to her, you bastard?'

Blair said wearily, 'Haven't any of your recent experiences taught you anything about jumping to conclusions?'

Robin ignored him, turning to Courtney. 'What's been going on?'

'Your erstwhile friend Mr Pallister has been here, that's all.' Courtney got to her feet, glad to find that the weakness had left her legs.

'Oh no!' Robin's face was appalled and guilty at

the same time. 'He—he wasn't violent, was he?'

'No,' she said. But she knew now that there was a violence more damaging, more frightening and destructive than pain and blows. She remembered the feel of that wet fleshy mouth sucking at hers, the rasping breath, the plump fingers exploring and squeezing, and a long shudder ran through her. She gave Rob a taut smile which held an element of reassurance. 'I'm going to have a bath. Will you excuse me, please.'

She felt ineffably weary as she lay in the warm scented water. The long wakeful night had taken its toll, and the events of the morning had almost crushed her. Almost but not quite.

She had plans to make. With Blair at Hunters Court, she and Robin would have to move away. It was impossible to stay under the circumstances. And she would go to Philip Carteret and ask him to take Rob back, although it was by no means certain that he would agree. One thing she knew, if the austere Mr Carteret discovered the extent of his godson's indebtedness to Monty Pallister, he would never again offer him any kind of employment. Nor was there the slightest possibility of him advancing Rob any money with which to pay Pallister off. She had discounted any such thought from the start.

She would have to try and raise a bank loan, although her heart failed her at trying to find an explanation for needing such an enormous sum of money which would satisfy a shrewd bank manager. And the repayments! How would she manage them when so much of her modest salary was already spoken for?

As she went into her bedroom, to find her hair drier, she heard to her relief the slam of the front door, and the sound of a car driving away a few moments later.

So Blair had gone, she thought thankfully. She sat on the edge of her bed, and dried the damp tips of her hair, fluffing it casually with her hand. An aroma of fresh coffee came tantalisingly up the stairwell and she sniffed at it appreciatively. Robin wasn't usually keen on even the simplest of domestic tasks. He was clearly eager to placate her in any way possible, she thought as she made her way down to the living room, still swathed in the ancient blue dressing gown which had been hers at boarding school.

She pinned on a determined smile as she pushed open the living room door. 'So you decided to make your own coffee,' she began teasingly, then stopped, biting back a gasp.

Blair was lounging in one of the chairs by the fire, his long legs stretched out to the warmth of the blazing logs. As his eyes swept over, a small derisive smile tugged at the corners of his mouth, and Courtney flushed hotly, her fingers moving hastily to the sash of her dressing gown to tighten it further round her slim waist.

'Where's Rob?' she demanded.

'He went out. He's gone to Wolverton to see your father.'

She smothered a groan of dismay. 'Why?'

He shrugged. 'Do you imagine you're the only one with any filial feelings? He has some bad news to break to him, and the sooner it's done, the better.'

A cry was wrung from her. 'What's he going to tell him? Doesn't he realise he has to break it to him gently—that another bad shock could ...' She choked on the possibility.

'Oh, for heaven's sake!' Blair's face was harsh as he rose and came to her side, taking her arm in a bruising grip. 'Give Rob credit for a modicum of common sense and sensitivity at least. He's hardly likely to pour out the whole mess to a sick man. Or do you imagine you have a monopoly of finer feelings?'

'Of course not,' she said raggedly. 'It's just that I thought Rob would want me to be there at least. He ...' She paused.

'He usually does,' he completed for her a trifle grimly. 'Between you, you and your father have never made it very easy for Rob to grow up, have you? No wonder Pallister found him such easy prey!'

'What's he been telling you?' Suddenly weary, Courtney allowed him to lead her forward to the sofa. She sank down on to the cushions, accepting the cup of coffee he poured for her with a murmured word of thanks.

'Everything,' he said briefly.

'I see.' Courtney was mortified. How could Robin have taken Blair into his confidence so easily?

'No, I don't think you do,' he said, pouring his own coffee. She noted that he took it black without sugar. 'There are times, Courtney, when a man needs someone other than a younger sister to confide in.'

'He has friends.'

'Then where are they?' he asked, his mouth twisting.

She didn't answer, just sat staring down at the swirl of fragrant liquid in her cup.

'Is the coffee not to your taste?' he enquired after a moment or two.

'It's fine,' she acknowledged stiffly. 'You certainly believe in making yourself at home.'

'Here?' he glanced round the room, and shook his head. 'You know better than that, Courtney. I now have a home of my own. I look forward to entertaining you there.'

'Then you're heading for a disappointment,' she said coldly. 'I'll never enter the house while you're there.'

He smiled slightly. 'I hope you'll change your mind. Otherwise it's going to add a considerable complication to my plans.'

She stared at him. 'And how can your plans possibly involve me?' She was annoyed with herself at betraying so much curiosity as soon as the words were uttered.

He said coolly, 'Because I intend to marry you.'

CHAPTER FIVE

HER hand jerked, and coffee splashed the old blue dressing gown.

She said dazedly, 'What did you say?'

'You heard me perfectly well.' Blair was leaning back in his chair again, apparently completely at ease, except for a slight narrowing of the hazel eyes as they watched her. 'I said I intend to make you my wife.'

'You're insane,' she said flatly.

He laughed out loud. 'You don't pay yourself any compliments, do you, darling?'

'You know what I meant,' she snapped. 'And don't call me "darling"!'

'What would you prefer I call you?'

'Nothing. Nothing at all. And now perhaps you'll get out of here.' She was flushed and trembling, her small breasts rising and falling rapidly in distress.

'Later,' he said. 'We'll have something to eat—I make a reasonable omelette—and then we'll go for a drive.'

'I wouldn't go to the end of the street with you!' she flashed stormily.

Blair shrugged equably. 'Then we'll stay here.' His eyes went over her, their gaze frankly sensual, leaving her with the disturbing feeling that the dressing gown had become transparent. 'In fact I'd prefer it,' he added, his voice deepening slightly.

Courtney banged her cup back on to the tray. 'This whole ridiculous discussion has gone on long enough,' she said angrily. 'Will you please leave? Unfortunately I'm not capable of throwing you out.'

'No,' he said. One hand went meditatively to the scar on his cheek. 'Throwing things at me is more your forte, as I have good reason to remember.'

'I hope you don't expect me to apologise for that,' she said defiantly.

'There are other ways of making amends,' he suggested silkily, and laughed again as colour warmed her face.

She said huskily, 'I only wish my aim had been better.'

'Think of all the practice you can have when we're married.'

'We're not going to be married. The suggestion is an outrage!'

'So, it seems, was the last idea I had about our relationship,' he said drily. 'I thought a respectable proposal would appeal to you more.'

'There is nothing about you that appeals to me, Blair Devereux,' she said between her teeth.

He gave her a long look. 'We both know that isn't true,' he reminded her quietly, and Courtney flinched inwardly at the recollection of the moments she had spent in his arms. She'd fought Monty Pallister, clawed him. Why couldn't she have done the same to Blair?

'Let's accept that you have a certain amount of expertise,' she said coldly. 'Nevertheless that does nothing to alter my basic feelings about you.'

'Which are?'

She took a breath. 'I hate you. I thought I'd already made that clear.'

'Don't be a child, Courtney.' His tone sounded almost bored. 'Marriage to me could solve a lot of your problems.'

'I fail to see how,' she said bitterly.

'Then think for a moment. The significance of that love scene I interrupted earlier hasn't been lost on me. I had my suspicions even before Rob told me that he owed Pallister money and was being pressured to repay it. So what was the deal? "'Be nice to me, little girl, and we'll say no more about it'"? Well, you wouldn't be the first, and certainly never the last. But no matter how "'nice'" you were, at the end of the day he'll still want his money, and you could end up earning it in ways you wouldn't like.'

Courtney repressed a shiver at the picture his quiet unemotional words conjured up. 'You could be right,' she allowed. 'But it will never happen, because I have not the slightest intention of being "nice" as you put it.'

'No? Then what will happen to Rob, if he can't repay the money? If you've convinced yourself that Pallister is bluffing, Courtney, then forget it. His sort doesn't make idle threats.'

'How dare you stand there, laying the law down!' Her voice held a trace of hysteria. 'It's because of you that Rob's in this situation.'

Blair lifted his eyebrows. 'Am I to blame because he couldn't handle a relatively simple job? I wasn't prepared to spend unlimited funds on acquiring Hunters Court. If Rob had gone on bidding, he would probably have won.'

'I'm sure that's a great consolation.' Her breathing quickened. 'But I don't believe you. I think you would have spent whatever it took to get Rob into trouble. Don't pretend you didn't know he was working for Monty Pallister.'

He shrugged. 'I knew—yes. Rob isn't particularly discreet, whether he knows it or not. But I didn't know the reason for his involvement until today.'

'And if you had known, would it have made any difference?'

'No.' The hazel eyes were direct and unsmiling. 'Rob shouldn't have left the shelter of Carteret's for the jungle, if he didn't know its laws.'

'You're well acquainted with them, of course!'

'I learned in one short, sharp lesson. Perhaps this experience will have the same salutory effect on your brother.'

'Which, naturally, was your intention all along,' Courtney said derisively.

'No,' he said. 'My only intentions all along were to buy the house and take you. They've been—obsessions with me for some time, and I didn't think beyond them.'

'Then perhaps you should have done,' she said

unsteadily. 'You're crazy to even imagine I would ever agree to marrying you.'

His mouth twisted slightly. 'I realised you might take some persuading.'

'Persuading?' Courtney gave a hard little laugh. 'Did you suppose I would fall into your arms after—a couple of kisses?'

'Hardly,' he said. 'We're not living in the last century. I'd figured a considerably closer relationship before you capitulated.'

'Then I suggest you think again,' she said coldly, trying to ignore the tinge of betraying colour which had crept into her face.

'I think about little else,' he said softly. 'Particularly under the stimulation of the knowledge that you haven't a stitch on under that garment.' His smile mocked her deepening flush. 'If you're planning to get dressed, now might be a good time. I'll have some lunch ready by the time you come downstairs, and then we'll go for that drive I mentioned.'

'I'm not going anywhere with you.'

'As you wish.' He shrugged out of his jacket, tossing it over the back of the chair. 'In that case, we'll stay here and make love.'

As he moved purposefully towards her, Courtney shot to her feet, her heart thumping.

'Don't you dare touch me!'

'Then do as you're told and put your clothes on.' He paused, hands on hips, only a couple of feet away. The set of his mouth was uncompromising. 'You have a count of three to make up your mind, or we take the first step towards that relationship I mentioned by ridding you of that dressing gown. One.'

For a long incredulous moment her eyes met his, seeking some hint of softening, of retraction. But there was none.

Instead Blair said quite gently, 'Two,' and took another step towards her.

The unthinkable suddenly became not just possible but probable.

Courtney said huskily, 'All right, you win. But I don't want anything to eat. It would choke me.'

The echo of his amused laugh pursued her as she fled to her room, almost tripping on the hem of her dressing gown on the stairs. She slammed the door, and for good measure wedged a chair under the handle. It was an overreaction, and she knew it, but she didn't care. Five minutes alone with him and any semblance of poise or rationality deserted her.

She sank down on the edge of the bed, wrapping her arms closely round her shaking body. Blair wanted to marry her. No, that sounded too tentative. Rather, he'd issued what sounded like a declaration of intent.

She shivered, remembering the unequivocal look in the hazel eyes as they had rested on her body. None of the casual relationships she had experienced so far had prepared her for the depth of sensual hunger she had glimpsed so disturbingly.

At the same time, she could hardly have expected to remain immune for ever. She wasn't a frigid type, or at least she'd never thought so, although there had been little opportunity to test the theory. She'd expected, one day, to be desired and to respond to that desire. But with the right man.

Not—ever—with Blair Devereux.

Ever since he had reappeared in their lives, he had delivered shock after shock, but he was wrong if he thought this constant pressure would rock her back on her heels. She would survive, somehow. She always had, she thought lifting her chin.

As she did so she caught sight of herself in the dressing-table mirror, and her reflection was hardly reassuring. She might be thinking brave thoughts, but she looked pale, large-eyed and vulnerable.

Half of it, of course, was because of this damned dressing gown, she told herself roundly, retrieving a handful of underwear. It might be relatively warm and comfortable, but it reduced her back to the status of a schoolgirl.

When she had finished dressing, the image was a far more satisfactory one. She had put on a high-necked cream sweater, teaming it with the soft flare of a navy wool skirt, and had fastened her dark hair back from her face with a pair of silver combs. She looked cool, and in control once more, no matter how uncertain she might feel inwardly.

Her own refusal of food had not deterred Blair from making a meal for himself, she realised, lips tightening as she entered the living room. It looked delicious as well, which didn't help—a large fluffy omelette, flavoured with a drift of melting cheese, and flanked by a pair of grilled tomatoes.

But she refrained from any more acid comments about his making himself at home. Experience had shown there was no future in that as a conversational gambit.

He looked up as she entered. 'Sure you won't change your mind?'

He might have meant about eating, or he might have meant—anything.

Courtney shook her head. 'Quite sure, thank you.' Which covered all the possibilities.

She seated herself on the sofa and picked up a newspaper, becoming absorbed in one of the feature articles to all intents and purposes.

Eventually Blair said, 'Are you ready?'

He had finished his meal and washed up, and was standing over her.

She said, 'I'm really not in the mood for outings. I want to be here when Rob comes back. We have things to discuss.'

'He won't be back for a while.' He leaned down, putting a hand under her elbow and assisting her none too gently to her feet. 'Plenty of time for what I have in mind. Do you need a jacket?'

Defeatedly, she fetched one—a quilted waistcoat in a warm, bright red.

'Ready?' he asked.

'If you say so,' she shrugged.

He said gently, 'Don't sulk, Courtney. It does nothing for you at all.'

She gave him a look of silent loathing as she walked past him out of the cottage to the car.

She'd intended to sit in stony silence, but that was before she realised the direction they were taking.

She stiffened. 'We're not . . .' she began.

'We are.' Blair didn't even glance at her. 'I'm going to look over my new possessions—or one of them at least.'

After a pause Courtney said glacially, 'I thought I'd made it quite clear . . .'

'You did,' he agreed, 'You spoke with admirable clarity, but I made no guarantees in return, or had you forgotten?'

She hadn't forgotten a thing. She sat rigid with temper as the car swept through the lanes, and turned in through the tall gates.

He parked in front of the house, and came round the passenger door.

'Out you get, darling,' he said coolly. 'Or do you want me to anticipate our wedding day by carrying you over the threshold?'

'No, thank you,' she muttered between gritted teeth.

The front door wasn't locked. It wasn't even shut, because Blair pushed it wide, and stood to one side to allow her to precede him into the hall. It took nearly all the courage she possessed to take that small step, but it had to be done, because she knew that his threat to carry her was no idle one, and the thought of being helpless in his arms was unbearable.

Once inside, she felt the house closing round her in welcome and a kind of comfort. She felt absurd tears pricking behind her eyelids, and prayed that Blair would not notice. She had never seen Hunters Court devoid of furniture before, and to her surprise it made the house seem smaller.

She looked around, missing details—the warm Turkey rugs on the flagged floor, the long side table with its collection of pewter. There was new paper too, she noticed, on the wall above the panelling—silky textured in shades of green and gold. Quite unlike the rather formal Jacobean design that had been there before, but she liked it.

As if he could read her thoughts, Blair said, 'I think this will do for the time being, don't you? We can start with the drawing room, and the master bedroom, and our bathroom, and get them right.'

'You must do what you wish—it's your house.' Her tone was clipped, but controlled.

'No,' he said, 'it's our house. You will live here with me, because that, my lovely Courtney, is what it's all about.'

She had begun to shake her head, protests welling up inside her fighting to be formed into words, when a girl's voice said, 'So there you are! I thought I heard the car.'

Courtney's head turned sharply in disbelief as Kate Lydyard emerged from the room that had been James Lincoln's study and walked across the hall to meet them.

She was smiling. She said, 'Hello, Courtney. It's been a long time.'

'Indeed it has,' Courtney managed.

Kate's smile widened. 'You look totally bemused. Hasn't Blair explained to you? No, of course he hasn't. Men are all the same. I've been working for him for over a year.'

She didn't look much like a working girl, Courtney thought with sudden waspishness. Her blonde hair was piled in an extravagant swirl on top of her head, and she was wearing a skirt, tunic and long boots in grey suede.

'You're his secretary?' Courtney asked doubtfully.

Kate's nose wrinkled slightly. 'Not quite. He has girls to do the shorthand and typing. I'm more his personal assistant.' She laughed. 'He still isn't convinced he needs me, so I'm out to make myself indispensable. To that end there's coffee in that room over there. Only out of a flask, I'm afraid, but better than nothing, especially as there's no heating on yet.' She turned to Blair, lowering her voice slightly. 'I found an old table in an outhouse at the back which I've brought in, to establish some sort of base. And I've brought the pattern books you wanted.'

They began to move towards the study, Courtney in the rear. She was frankly bewildered by this new turn of events.

Kate Lydyard, of all people! She hadn't seen or heard anything of her or from her since that last summer holiday. Not that that had surprised her. Between the Courtney Lincoln whose family owned Hunters Court, and who attended St Adela's school, and the girl who'd been forced to earn some kind of living after a widely reported financial scandal, there was an unbridgeable gulf, or there would be as far as Kate was concerned. Not all the girls she'd mixed with in the sixth form had felt the same. She was still in touch with Anna Harper, for one.

But she'd certainly never expected that Kate would cross her path again, and especially in the present circumstances.

As she walked into the study, Kate was already pouring the coffee into paper cups.

'I've drawn up a provisional staff list,' she was saying. 'I presume Mrs Garvin will be coming here with you.' She handed Courtney one of the cups. Her mouth was still smiling, but the blue eyes were shrewd and assessing, taking in everything she needed to know. 'Have you met Mrs Garvin, Courtney?' She took the negative for granted and went on almost without a pause. 'Blair's angel. The sort of cook-housekeeper that one only imagines exists.'

She picked up a clipboard from the small square table which stood rather forlornly in the centre of the room. 'The outside staff should be no problem—most of them have been here for years—all local people. Will you be wanting to make any changes?' She looked at Blair, her brows lifted questioningly.

He shrugged. 'Probably not. I've never seen the place

looking anything but immaculate. But I'll need some additional people—a groom and an assistant for starters. Again I'd like locals to be made the offer first. Perhaps we could make some enquiries before advertising.' He glanced across at Courtney, standing motionless holding her untouched coffee. 'Unless you know someone, Courtney.'

She shook her head. 'Not a soul,' she lied expressionlessly.

There was a brief, sharp silence, broken by Kate.

'It doesn't matter,' she said with a lift of one shoulder. 'I'll ask around. That's often the best way.'

They went on talking. Blair had moved to Kate's side and was standing, one hand on her shoulder looking down at the papers on the clipboard, nodding occasionally and interpolating comments.

Courtney didn't hear what they were saying. She didn't want to hear. All her attention was concentrated with almost frightening force on the room itself. She could see her father's desk in front of the window, see her father almost crouching in his chair, his face white and drawn as he tried to defend himself from the bitter aggression being hurled at him.

The only voices she could hear were his and Blair's—shouting, accusation being followed by counter-accusation, Blair's threatening. And then her own voice, crying out, her hand reaching for the ashtray in a desperate attempt to silence those accusations.

'What the hell's the matter? You look like a ghost!' Blair's voice brought her harshly back to reality.

She gasped, moving abruptly, spilling the coffee down her skirt.

'Oh dear!' Kate was at her side, solicitous with a handkerchief. 'What a shame! Such a lovely skirt.'

'It will clean,' Courtney said shortly. She turned to Blair. 'Will we be getting back soon? I—I'm not feeling very well.'

'Another headache?' He was watching her sardonically. 'Or a recurrence of this morning's symptoms?'

'Neither.' She didn't bother to dissemble, ignoring the speculative glance from Kate. 'But if you don't mind, I'll get some fresh air.'

It had stopped raining, but the air on the terrace was raw and damp, filled with the scent of wet earth. Courtney leaned against the stone balustrade, feeling its chill penetrate her flesh, but it could not equal the chill within her.

Just then, in the study, she had felt real pain, and it had left her aching and confused. Because for the first time she had remembered everything about that terrible evening, and not just what she allowed herself to remember.

With total recall, she knew now that she hadn't been wholly her father's defender, as she'd always told herself since. That she had stood there between them that night, almost torn in two by her feelings. Love and loyalty to her father had combated—what? New emotions towards Blair, fragile and agonising in their intensity.

She had no thought of taking sides. All she'd wanted to do was scream at them to stop because they were tearing her to pieces. Ever since she had first heard about Geoffrey Devereux, ever since the news of his arrest had come through, she had known there would be this conflict, and she had been terrified at its prospect. It had taken the future she had begun to make plans about, all the secret dreams, and turned them upside down, leaving her floundering in a welter of emotional uncertainty.

She had taken her father's side, of course, because it was inevitable that she should do so. The white, sick look he had worn had frightened her, arousing all her protective instincts, withering and blighting whatever she might have been capable of feeling for Blair.

Besides, there'd been so little to build on—a kiss, and the gift of a rose. Nothing else, except the promise of his return. Far too delicate a foundation to survive the kind of storm that followed.

And ever since it had been easier, simpler to hate,

and to feed the memory of hostility.

Easier, that was, until Blair had kept his promise and come back. Courtney hadn't bargained for that. She had taken it for granted that he was out of her life for ever. That the last words between them had been spoken. And she'd wanted it that way, because there could be no other. The rose had died, shedding its petals, and she'd thrown it away. Finis.

But now everything had changed, and she was frightened again, and uncertain. Thankfully this time she was older, wiser, able to fight the fear and confusion.

The instinct which had driven her to her father's support had been the right one, and he still needed her. That was all she needed to remember from the past and into the future. That was still the same.

Behind her, Blair said drily, 'Feeling better?'

Courtney took a deep, calming breath before she turned to face him.

'A little.'

'I'm staying here for a while,' he said. 'I've got decorators moving in shortly, so there are decisions that have to be made. I'd hoped you'd help me make them.' He paused, but she made no response, and after a moment his lips tightened. 'Kate has her car here. She'll take you back to the cottage, if that's what you want?'

'It's what I want,' she agreed flatly.

He smiled faintly. 'So you're prepared to trust my judgment over how the house should be decorated.'

'I trust nothing about you at all.' She met his gaze levelly. 'But fortunately Hunters Court is no longer any concern of mine. Do what you want with it. I'm not interested.'

'Bravely spoken,' he approved cynically. 'You've never let truth interfere with a point you wanted to make, have you, Courtney? I'll see you later.'

'No!' The word sounded harsh and raw, but she was past caring. 'How can I get it across to you? I don't want to see you again, Blair. You must—you must leave me alone.'

The hazel eyes were bleak as they looked her over.
There wasn't a trace of amusement left in him.

He said very quietly, 'Unfortunately, as we both
know, that's impossible.'

He went back into the house, leaving her alone.

Kate's car was a Metro, the latest registration and top
of the range, Courtney noted drily. She was a confident,
if aggressive, driver too.

As they turned out of the gates, she said, 'Pity you
aren't well. It must be a strange sensation, visiting your
old home, and knowing that it belongs to someone
else.'

'But hardly a novelty,' Courtney pointed out steadily.
'It's been occupied over the past three years by someone
else.'

Kate sent her a smiling sidelong glance. 'Not exactly
in the same way, I'd have thought.' She paused. 'It must
bring back a lot of memories.'

Courtney shrugged. 'I've never been a nostalgia buff,'
she returned. 'One of the things I remember best is how
much it cost to run. I wish Blair joy of his purchase.'

'Oh, I don't imagine the costs will present much
problem.' Kate slowed for a sharp bend, but not much.
'Blair is a very wealthy man, as you must know.'

That had been almost too casually thrown away,
Courtney thought grimly. And what was she supposed
to say in return, admit her ignorance and plead for
enlightenment?

'Over my dead body,' she thought.

Aloud, she said, 'I suppose he is,' which could mean
anything. After a pause, she added with a smile, 'Is that
how you come to be working for him?'

During their schooldays when they had all talked
about the future, Kate had already had her sights set
firmly on a career where money was.

Kate overtook a small van with finesse. If there was a
hesitation it was only a brief one, and could have been
because she was concentrating on her driving.

She said, 'We met at a party, as it happens. I was

working in public relations at the time, and getting nowhere fast, so when Blair suggested he might have a job for me I was more than interested.' There was a note which was hard to define in her voice as she added, 'So far, it's worked out very well.'

'I'm pleased to hear it,' Courtney said noncomittally. She wasn't expecting Kate to ask how she was leading her life these days, and she wasn't disappointed. Kate hadn't been surprised to see her when she arrived at the house, so presumably, working for Blair, she already knew whatever she needed to know.

But there were other elements she might not be aware of. Did Kate know, Courtney wondered, that Blair had spoken to her of marriage? Somehow she doubted it. Kate had not been one of those who had thrown herself openly at Blair during that long warm summer holiday, but that had not implied any lack of interest on her part. She'd always seemed so much older than the rest of them, so much more sophisticated, and this had just been part of that sophistication.

And now she was working for him. As his personal assistant, she had been necessarily close to him for over a year. She was too clever to be obvious, but at the same time Courtney doubted whether she would have let any grass grow under her feet.

So far, it's worked out very well,' she'd said. From which it could be inferred that she had hopes of even greater things in the future.

She may not have been surprised to see me, Courtney thought, but she wasn't pleased either. She probably thought once the house was sold to the Hallorans that we'd have moved far away from here. And I wish now that we had.

At the time, staying had seemed the most sensible course. The offer of the cottage, her job, the proximity to Wolverton and the nursing home, and the fact the village was within commuting distance to London for Robin, had all been factors which counted in the final decision.

Yet if she'd known that Blair would ever return, she

would have run far and fast, and found somewhere to hide, she thought bitterly.

It wasn't too late. The trust which owned the nursing home had others in different parts of the country. She wouldn't be able to afford the kind of accommodation she had at the moment, but that was a sacrifice she was prepared to make. Other girls survived, and more, in bedsitters. Why shouldn't she?

'I'm going to need directions.' Kate's crisp voice drew her attention to the fact that they had just passed the village signpost.

'Along the main street, and left at the T-junction.' Courtney took a breath. 'Thank you for driving me back. I know how busy you must be.'

'It's all part of the day's work.' Kate's cool tone cancelled any faint vestiges of warmth lingering from the old days at school. They'd never been close friends, but now they were to be less than acquaintances, it seemed.

Courtney said, 'It's the last house on the right—the one with the red door.'

Kate drew up smoothly outside, but made no attempt to switch off the engine. 'So this is home,' she commented. 'Quite a contrast.' She was clever, but not quite astute enough to conceal the evident note of satisfaction in her voice. Or perhaps she just didn't care, thought Courtney.

She said, 'That's it,' in cheerful agreement. 'Thanks again for the lift. I'm sure you're in a hurry to get back.'

Now either of them were in any doubt about the other's attitude, she thought wryly as the Metro turned neatly and sped off. And she had another potential enemy to add to a lengthening list.

With a defeated sigh, she turned and went into the cottage.

CHAPTER SIX

WHERE Robin was waiting.

He looked pale and unhappy, Courtney noticed instantly, and her heart contracted.

'How did Daddy take the news?' she demanded.

'All right,' he said, clearing his throat. 'I didn't tell him everything, of course. Just that there'd been a higher bid, so the whole deal was off.'

'You didn't stay long,' she commented, glancing at the clock on the mantelpiece.

'There wasn't a great deal to stay for,' Robin said defensively. 'Besides, he was expecting the therapist.' He swallowed. 'On the way back I stopped at the pub to see Monty.'

Courtney had knelt on the rug to add another log to the fire. She dusted her hands together slowly. 'And?'

'What do you expect? He's bloody furious,' he flung at her sullenly. 'Why the hell did you have to go off the deep end like that?'

She turned, giving him an incredulous stare. 'You mean I should have stood there and let him maul me to his heart's content? Rob...'

'Oh, be your age. I owe the man money!'

'So he's permitted to collect anything on account from me?' Dull colour entered her face. 'Have you any idea what you're saying?'

'I don't mean—that.' Robin flushed too. 'But Courtney, you could have—played him along somehow, couldn't you? Kept him sweet at least. As it is——' he groaned, burying his face in his hands. His voice was muffled as he said, 'I have to find the money by the end of next week, otherwise I'm going to be damaged. Those were his own words. He didn't specify how.'

He didn't need to, Courtney thought, compassionately viewing Rob's bowed head. The implication in the threat was the stuff nightmares were made of.

She said, trying to keep her voice level, 'Then we'll have to find the money somehow.'

After a pause he said, 'Did Blair say anything?'

'About what?' In spite of herself, she could feel the colour run slow and hot under her skin.

Robin shrugged helplessly. 'About the mess I'm in.'

'Not a great deal,' she said. 'Whatever possessed you to confide in him?'

'Because he's got money,' Rob came back grimly. 'It may even be our money.'

Courtney shook her head. 'There's no point in hoping for help from Blair,' she said quietly.

'How do we know if we don't ask? Besides, he owes us this after all he's done to us.'

Courtney recognised wryly the shift in emphasis. It was no longer just Rob's problem. It was hers to share.

'I doubt if he'd see it that way. Stop thinking like that, Rob. It will get us nowhere.'

'So what other ideas do you have? Apologising to Monty, maybe. From what he said, you'd have to grovel.'

'No.' Her mouth twisted in revulsion. 'That's out of the question.'

The sullen look had returned. 'Then you think of something.'

She thought about nothing else for the duration of that endless weekend. The telephone rang twice, and she answered it each time with a feeling of panic gripping her stomach. The first time, it was Philip Carteret asking with a certain coolness whether Robin could be expected back at his desk on Monday or not. Courtney set herself to soothe him, offering him some kind of explanation for Robin's recent conduct, and promising more reliable behaviour in the future. On the second occasion it was Clive, asking her to go out with him, but she made an excuse. An evening spent swapping social nothings was beyond her.

From Blair she heard nothing.

On Monday she dispatched a protesting Robin off to Wolverton to catch the London train, and went to her own office as usual. There was a lot of correspondence to catch up with now that her boss had returned, and she was glad to be kept too busy to think.

During the lunch hour she visited the bank and asked to see the manager. He was kind but firm. With her present salary, and lack of adequate sureties, and bearing in mind the current interest rates, the loan she requested was impossible. Now if she wanted a small sum for a holiday, perhaps, or towards a new car . . .

She thanked him and came away, aware for the first time just how much she had counted on persuading him to agree. It was as if a door had just been slammed on her, and for a moment she stood in the street looking around her as if she had suddenly opened her eyes to find herself in a foreign country.

A hand took her arm and Blair said sharply, 'Courtney? What is it? Are you ill?'

She pulled herself free. 'No, of course not.'

He looked down at her frowning. 'You look like hell,' he said bluntly. 'Have you stopped eating and sleeping?'

'Let's just say I have things on my mind.'

'And feeding yourself clearly isn't one of them. You're coming with me.' This time the grip on her arm was too firm to dislodge, and she couldn't struggle without making a scene. Fuming silently, she allowed herself to be guided into the lounge of the Angel Hotel in the market place. She refused all offers of alcohol because she had to go back to work that afternoon, accepting only a tomato juice. But she could not be so strong-minded about the menu which Blair handed her. The Angel's home-made meat pies were justly famous, and she had been neglecting her diet lately, it was true. A robust plateful of carbohydrates might put this dreadful inner shakiness to flight.

She finally put her knife and fork down on her empty plate with the guilty suspicion that she had just made a pig of herself, and half expecting some satirical comment from Blair. But none was forthcoming. He merely ordered coffee, and a brandy for himself after checking that she wouldn't join him.

She poured cream into her cup, and stirred it round, more for something to do than anything else. The food hadn't helped that feeling of unease at all, she'd discovered, and she knew why.

It was Blair who filled her with this tense, trembling awareness, even in a public place like the lounge of the Angel. Not that it was so very public, she thought, looking round her. Customers wanting lunch on this cold damp Monday were thin on the ground. She and Blair were almost isolated in their corner.

He said, 'I called at the cottage earlier. I'd forgotten you were a working lady.'

'Oh.' She didn't look at him, her fingers fiddling nervously with the spoon in her saucer.

'Oh,' he echoed mockingly. 'I came to see whether you'd made a decision yet.'

'I don't understand. A decision about what?' Even to herself, her voice sounded breathless.

'You understand perfectly well,' he returned equably. 'A decision about our marriage.'

She said hoarsely, 'I thought I'd already made it plain I wasn't prepared to marry you.'

'I thought you might have had second thoughts.'

'No,' said Courtney, swallowing. 'Frankly, I'd rather die.'

'And Rob? What sort of fate do you visualise for him when whatever time limit he's been set finally runs out? No, wait.' He lifted a silencing hand as she began defensively to protest. 'I saw where you were coming from earlier, Courtney, and you looked as if you'd been poleaxed. I could have told you the kind of answer to expect, if I thought it would have done any good.'

'Of course,' she said, 'you're a very wealthy man now—Kate told me. You'll know all the ins and outs of the world of finance.'

Blair said wearily, 'I don't pretend to. But it wouldn't take a financial genius to guess what any bank manager in his right mind would think of the kind of deal you were offering.'

Courtney stared at the polished surface of the table they were sitting at. She and Robin had talked endlessly over the weekend, exploring possibilities, but every discussion had seemed to end with Rob saying, 'Blair's got the money.'

She said quietly, 'So you're offering me a deal of your own?'

'Yes,' he said. 'I think Robin's behaved like a fool, and ordinarily I'd be tempted to let him stew. But my brother-in-law would be a different case altogether. I don't want him ending up on crutches or worse.'

'Like your father-in-law,' she said bleakly. 'Or had you forgotten about him? What effect do you imagine it would have on him if I agreed to your monstrous proposition?'

'He's more resilient than you give him credit for,' Blair said coolly. 'As it happens, I went to see him yesterday.'

'You did *what*?' Her eyes were enormous as she gazed at him. 'Why?'

'To talk,' he said. 'To tell him, among other things, that I've bought Hunters Court, and why.'

Her voice was low and shaken. 'If you've upset him— made him ill again . . .'

'I told you he was resilient. He's also a realist. He always knew I'd be back, so he wasn't altogether surprised to see me. Not pleased, you understand, but not astonished either. Perhaps Rob's stumbling explanations from the day before had set some kind of mental early warning system working.'

There were two bright spots of colour in her face. She exclaimed, 'How dare you do such a thing!'

He shrugged. 'It didn't take much daring. I'm the nephew of the man who was once his partner and his closest friend.'

'The man who robbed him blind and ruined him,' she said fiercely.

Blair said slowly, 'Unless there's been an intrinsic

change in the law in this country, a man is still innocent until proved guilty. The charges against my uncle were never substantiated.'

'Because he cheated the law!'

There was a sudden blaze in the hazel eyes, but his voice remained level. 'That's something we're hardly likely to agree on.'

'There are numerous things in that category.' Courtney took a deep breath. 'We're on opposite sides—you must see that. Or do you expect me just to—forget the past.'

'Why should I? I haven't forgotten. I loved my uncle, and I believed in him. I believe in him still, enough to think that if he'd lived, he'd have cleared his name, somehow. I want to see that name re-established—respected. The kind of public reconciliation with your family that our marriage would imply is only the first step.'

She stared at him. 'You really think that?'

'I do. But that isn't the only reason. I need a wife to run my home, to act as my hostess. You know the house, and you know that kind of life.'

She said, 'So does Kate Lydyard.'

'That's true,' he said mockingly. 'But she lacks one prime asset—that of being James Lincoln's daughter. He'll be well enough to leave the nursing home before too long, so he can move in with us at Hunters Court.'

'You really hate us, don't you?' she whispered. 'You want to make us suffer . . .'

'Suffer?' Blair's mouth curled sardonically. 'Giving you back your family home to live in, rescuing your brother from debt, providing your father with a roof over his head. I thought I was being magnanimous.'

Silence closed round her achingly. At last Courtney said, 'And if I agree to live in your house, to be your hostess, you'll give Rob the money he needs.'

'Yes. Do I take that as your consent?'

'I seem to have little choice,' she said bitterly.

'There is an alternative, of course,' he told her. 'You could throw yourself on friend Pallister's tender mercies. But judging by your previous reaction, you'd probably prefer my bed to his.'

She gave him a steady look. 'That's purely academic, of course. I've said I'll be your hostess. But I won't be anything else.'

She didn't know how Blair would react. He might well refuse to pay the money unless she changed her mind, she thought, bracing herself for conflict.

Something flared briefly behind his eyes and vanished. He gave a short laugh and drank the remains of his coffee.

'If that's what you want,' he said with a dismissive lift of his shoulder. 'Just as long as you don't expect to impose some kind of celibate existence on me, darling, because it won't work.'

'Of course not.' Courtney lifted her chin. 'You'd be free to do whatever you wanted.'

'As long as I leave you alone,' he added, and laughed again. 'All right, Courtney. I'll be satisfied with having the Lincoln family in the palm of my hand as my pensioners—for the time being, anyway. Who knows? One of these nights, you may change your mind, and then I'll be waiting.'

'You'll wait for ever,' she said.

'Now that has a familiar ring.' He still sounded amused. 'Have you got to fly back to your office, or have we time to buy you an engagement ring?'

She glanced at her watch and gasped. 'I'm late already!'

'But as you're going to be handing your notice in anyway, that hardly matters,' Blair told her.

'But surely there's no need——' she began, only to be cut off by his incisive, 'There's every need. The wedding's going to take place as soon as it can be arranged. So you tell your boss today that you're leaving at the end of the week. I'll be back then, to talk over details with you.'

'Where are you going?' He had got to his feet, and she rose too.

'To London—to see Robin and arrange to pay off

Pallister. That's the whole purpose of the exercise, isn't it—from your point of view?'

'Yes.' Courtney bit her lip, then said rapidly, 'Blair, please don't do this. Please just—lend me the money. I'll pay it back somehow, I swear I will—only . . .'

'Oh, you'll pay, darling,' he said softly. 'You'll pay for everything—and with interest.'

His hands reached out and took her shoulders, jerking her towards him. His mouth fastened on hers so savagely that for a dazed moment she couldn't breathe.

When he let her go, her face was ashen, her only colour in her bruised lips. She could only be thankful that the other tables were now deserted, and even the barmaid was missing from her usual place, so there had been no one to witness his embrace.

He smiled grimly, as if he could read her thoughts. 'Something to remember me by,' he said. 'Until the weekend.'

Courtney watched him cross to the door and disappear, then sank back on to her seat. She had to calm herself.

She couldn't go back to the offiice in this state. She lifted tentative fingers to her sensitive mouth, wincing a little, but the pain she felt wasn't physical.

In spite of Blair's harshness, something unbidden deep within her had leaped to life at the first pressure of his lips on hers.

After a while, a waitress came to clear the table, sending Courtney a rather curious glance, but she was quite oblivious, sunk in a bleak and disturbing little world of her own.

She hardly dared contemplate the future she had brought upon herself. Even the possibility of returning to live at Hunters Court could not balance out the inevitable bitterness which would follow.

She shivered. Couldn't Blair see that what he was trying to do was impossible? Geoffrey Devereux had been a thief and a betrayer, and no stage-managed reconciliation between Blair and the Lincolns was going to make the slightest difference. The truth would always be there, dividing them, keeping them hostile strangers under the same roof.

Courtney bit her lip. Why couldn't Blair accept that he had been as much deceived by his uncle as they had themselves? By forcing his way back into their lives like this, he was simply re-opening old wounds. And creating fresh ones, she thought in a kind of anguish.

What was this strange marriage, yet not a marriage, he was determined to foist on her? Her impulsive stipulation that he should make no demands on her as his wife had been accepted without a second thought. And yet—and yet that had not been his original intention, and she knew it.

She sighed. Everything came second to this strange obsession with his uncle's good name—even physical desire. He would be satisfied by their dependence on him, by the appearance of amity that the marriage and her father's presence at Hunters Court would bestow. But would she?

The question stung at her brain as she walked back to the office. Once there, she apologised for her tardiness and delivered her amazing news with a total absence of emotion.

She couldn't complain about the way it was received. A bottle of sherry was produced, while everyone crowded round her in laughing congratulations, and the working afternoon turned into a celebration.

'When's the wedding?' someone demanded. 'And where are you and Clive going to live?'

Courtney put her glass down, feeling colour sweep into her face. It was a natural enough mistake. She and Clive had been seen together enough, she supposed, to be regarded as a couple, and all she'd told Arthur Lloyd, her boss, was that she was leaving to be married.

She forced a smile. 'Clive and I were never that serious,' she said. 'I'm marrying someone I've known for years—Blair Devereux.'

'Devereux,' Mr Lloyd repeated after a pause. His face was a study. Courtney could see him remembering back three years, and his bewilderment deepening to a rather touching anxiety.

Other people had memories too. She could see glances being exchanged, shrugs, and gradually everyone returned to work, rather to her relief. She got on well with the other girls, but was not close enough to any of them to warrant any searchingly intimate questions about this new relationship, and she was thankful for this.

At the end of the afternoon when she took the folder of letters into Mr Lloyd's room for signature, he gave her a rather restrained smile.

He said, 'There's an old saying, Courtney, about marrying in haste. Like most clichés it still has an element of truth. I hope you're not doing that.'

'I don't think so,' she said. 'As I mentioned earlier, I've known Blair a long time.'

'Yes, but— —' Mr Lloyd paused, at a loss how to continue. 'Well, all I can do is wish you joy, my dear, and hope everything works out.'

Courtney smiled and murmured something which she hoped sounded both joyous and reassuring, although she doubted it.

She had a raging headache by the time she reached the cottage that evening. She made herself a makeshift meal of some cold meat and salad, and went to bed early, but not to sleep.

Instead she tossed and turned miserably, telling herself over and over again that it was not her fault, that she'd had no real choice. Rob was her brother and she loved him. She had had to do whatever was necessary to save him from disaster, even if the solution could only mean catastrophe for herself.

But what else could she do? she asked herself. Robin was safe now, and that had to be her comfort, but it was a very small gain when weighed in the balance against all the difficulties crowding towards her.

There was one forlorn hope. Perhaps Blair would decide, once he had considered the matter rationally and at a distance, that he had no wish to be confined in the kind of sterile relationship they were committed to. Courtney still couldn't understand why he hadn't offered any kind of protest about her sudden ultimatum. After all, he had made it more than clear previously that he—desired her.

She felt her face burn as she recalled those taut moments in the car when she had responded with mindless urgency to his kiss. He had wanted her then— and since—which made his cool acceptance of her refusal to sleep with him all the more surprising.

Not that she should question it, she thought. She could only be relieved that he had reacted as he had. Because if he had insisted on claiming his rights, he would ultimately have discovered the secret that she had at all costs to guard—that she was in love with him.

Even admitting it to herself was a painful thing. She had fought against it for so long, despising herself for still being prey to what could only be a girlish infatuation. She had told herself repeatedly that it was over. It had to be over, because there was no future in it, and never had been. Each time she had thought about him, she had deliberately whipped herself into rage, remembering the violent bitterness of their last meeting, crushing down the feeling of desolation which always lurked on the edge of her consciousness, the awareness that circumstances had conspired to rob her of something unutterably precious and exciting.

Eventually she supposed she would have forgotten about it, or at least stopped hurting when she remembered. Eventually, too, there would have been someone else. She had promised herself that.

Only Blair had come back, and she knew now how futile all her efforts had been, because here she was lost and totally vulnerable, and about to be more bitterly hurt than she had ever dreamed possible.

She was thankful that he had never shown her anything approaching the tenderness of that first kiss in the rose garden, because if he had then she would have been completely defeated. As it was, even the brush of his hand, the slide of those cool hazel eyes down her body sent her pulses racing dizzily, and the blood singing in her veins.

It was as well he'd returned not for love, but for vengeance, because at least that left her with some defences.

Courtney sighed, burying her unhappy face in a pillow which suddenly seemed to have been stuffed with red-hot bricks.

But those defences would last only as long as she could hold him at arms' length, and as a little sob rose in her throat, Courtney realised she had little faith in her ability, or her resolve, to do any such thing.

It was one of the most difficult weeks she had ever spent. At the office, her engagement continued to be something of a nine-day wonder, and Courtney was aware by the sudden silence and embarrassed looks that it was being discussed almost each time she turned her back, and that the events of three years ago were being endlessly resurrected. Not that she could have expected a great deal else, she thought wryly.

She found she needed to take her courage in both hands to break the news to Clive, who began by refusing flatly to believe her, and ended by being quite justifiably sullen and angry, slamming out of the cottage with scarcely a goodbye. This saddened her. She would have liked to have remained friends, although she would never have come anywhere near falling in love with him. She didn't think Clive had any serious feelings about her either. It was simply that his pride was hurt.

She had a cool interview with his father when he called later in the week to collect the monthly rent.

'I understand you'll be giving notice shortly,' was the Colonel's opening remark.

Courtney said quietly, 'I'm afraid I can't tell you exactly what my plans are at the moment, Colonel, but I shall eventually be going back to live at Hunters Court.'

'Hm.' Colonel FitzHugh's grunt was sharp with disapproval. 'No doubt you know your own mind,

Courtney, but it seems an extraordinary business—
quite extraordinary.'

He refused the cup of coffee she offered, and went off
without his usual friendly chat.

The following evening she went to Wolverton to see
her father. He had just finished supper when she
arrived, and was sitting in a chair, an unread book lying
in his lap. The face he turned to the door as she entered
looked drawn and weary, and his greeting seemed even
more stilted than dictated by his disability.

Speaking over-brightly, she congratulated him on his
progress, teasing him about his therapist's attractions,
but although he smiled and replied in kind, it was
clearly an effort, and for the first time tension lay
between them like a stone.

At last she broke the awkward silence. 'I've something
to tell you, Daddy. I'm afraid it may be rather a shock.
I—I'm going to be married.'

He nodded slowly, his eyes heavy as they rested on
her face.

'It's Blair Devereux.' It was a statement, rather than
a question.

Courtney caught her breath. 'How did you know? He
hasn't . . .?'

'He hasn't been back here? No, my dear. I may be
paralysed, but my wits still work. When there's nothing
to do but think, things fall into place.' He looked past
Courtney, his face suddenly remote and guarded in an
odd way. 'I think I always knew—always was afraid of
this. Years ago I was aware—that he wanted the
house—that he wanted you.' His voice died away, and
he seemed to withdraw even further into some
disturbing inner world.

Courtney said rapidly, 'Daddy, you must let me
explain why . . .'

He lifted his good hand, smiling faintly. 'There isn't
any need, darling. My brains haven't gone begging, as I
said just now. It's Robin, isn't it? I knew when he was
here the other day that there was something very
wrong, but he didn't confide in me, and I didn't probe.

I hoped he might be able to work it out for himself, but I was wrong. Blair had to rescue him, and you had to pay the price.' He paused, looking at her sadly. 'Don't tell me if I'm right—I need some illusions. I'd like to think my daughter was marrying the man she loved—and for the right reasons.'

She said, 'Yes,' in a subdued voice, because it was impossible to tell him the truth. Her father, of all people, would never understand how she could have fallen in love with the man who should have been her mortal enemy. There was a terrible disloyalty in that, and she could not hurt her father by confessing it.

After a pause, she said, 'At least we'll be living at Hunters Court again,' and tried to smile. 'Everything has its compensations.'

'Yes,' her father said quietly. 'I thought I'd never see the house again.' He was silent for a moment, then, 'I never meant this to happen, Courtney. You must believe that. If it hadn't been for this damned stroke, I'd have brought us round somehow. I—I never wanted you to be—sacrificed.'

She looked at him in surprise. She had never heard him speak in that way before—with such passion in his voice, and something underlying the passion which she could not quite analyse. He had always seemed resigned to their change in fortunes.

Now he added heavily, 'Oh God, it's all my fault.'

'You mustn't say that,' Courtney protested uneasily. 'It isn't true. You couldn't legislate for being ill—or for anything else.' She hesitated for a moment. 'And it must be awful to know someone for years, to trust them implicitly and then find out they've betrayed you in the worst way. You couldn't guard against that.'

The drawn, sick look was back. After a long silence he said, 'No.'

Courtney picked up her bag. She said, 'You look tired, and I know I've upset you. But I had to tell you myself. You had to know.'

He forced a smile. 'You could never upset me, darling. And I knew already.' His eyes remote again suddenly. 'I knew when he came back. There could be no other explanation.'

As she drove back to the cottage, Courtney's mind revolved everything that had been said over and over again. Her father's reaction had been surprising, even if he had been to some extent forewarned by Blair's visit. She'd expected anger and bitterness, demands for full explanations. Yet except for that one brief time when he had spoken of her being 'sacrificed', there had been little emotion in his reception of her news. Blair had said he was resilient, she thought, and it seemed he was right. It was worrying that he should have assessed James Lincoln more accurately than she had done herself. He was an outsider, and yet he could make them all dance to his tune like puppets.

As the weekend approached, she felt herself becoming on edge at the prospect of seeing Blair again. Her heart-searching had done her no good at all, she thought bitterly. It would have been easier to continue with the delusion that she hated him than just to pretend.

As she rather wearily prepared her evening meal on Friday she found she was listening half the time for the sound of a car coming down the lane.

But when the front door did open unceremoniously, it was to admit Rob.

He gave her a shamefaced look and muttered, 'Oh, there you are.'

'Where did you think I'd be?' she asked reasonably.

He shrugged. 'Under the circumstances—perhaps at Hunters Court.'

'So you know,' she said quietly.

'Of course I know,' he said sullenly. 'I had it from your future husband himself. He was extremely frank on exactly why he was lending the money, and what his conditions were. He's a bastard! He made me feel about—ten years old,' he added furiously.

Courtney said rather unsteadily, 'Rob, I'm sorry, but there seemed no other way.'

'I don't know why he simply couldn't have lent us the

money,' he said resentfully. 'Although I admit I'm thankful to have Monty off my back, I didn't bargain to replace him with Blair, yet that's what's happened.'

His tone said loud and clear that he blamed her for this, and Courtney repressed a sigh as she sprinkled the top of her cottage pie with cheese and popped it under the grill to brown.

Resentment didn't seem to have spoiled his appetite. He ate more than his share, and was plainly put out that there was nothing more substantial than fruit and cheese to follow.

'I suppose your culinary abilities will be wasted once you're married to Blair,' he remarked as she cleared the table. 'Does he even know that you can cook?'

'I don't think the subject ever came up,' she said coolly, carrying the used plates through to the kitchen. Rob followed, leaning in the doorway, his eyes speculative.

'I'd like to know what was discussed,' he said. 'The topic of your old school friend Kate Lydyard, for instance. Did he mention her?'

Courtney filled the sink with hot water and added a judicious amount of washing up liquid.

'If you're going to tell me that she works for him, please don't bother. I already know it,' she said rather shortly. She reached into a drawer for a clean tea towel, and tossed it to him. 'You can help.'

He grimaced, but came over to stand beside the draining board.

'Oh yes, she works for him,' he said, and laughed. 'A very close and confidential post, by all accounts. Just how personal an assistant do you have to be, I wonder, for the boss to pay the rent on your flat?'

'I've no idea.' Courtney rinsed a glass with more than ordinary care. 'Why don't you ask Blair, if you really want to know?'

'I'd have thought you were the person to do that. It seems to me like the sort of thing a wife would want to know.'

She shrugged, dumping a handful of cutlery into the

draining basket. 'Perhaps, when I'm a wife, I will. Blair is free to do what he wants in the meantime.' And afterwards, she added silently, with a pang that struck her to the heart. Despising herself, she went on casually, 'How did you discover all this?'

Robin shrugged. 'I had to visit his offices several times.' His eyes narrowed slightly. 'A penthouse suite— very glamorous. No shortage of money, but then we knew that, didn't we? I suppose we should be pleased to know that he's making the most of his ill-gotten gains. Anyway, he's got a pretty receptionist, and I took her out for a drink one evening. I don't think La Lydyard is exactly her favourite person.'

Courtney said coldly, 'If she's that indiscreet, I'd say Blair needed a new receptionist. And please don't say any more about ill-gotten gains. I'm going to marry Blair and I don't like . . .'

'And I don't like to know that my sister is for sale to him like everything else,' Robin said harshly. 'Why didn't you tell him to go to hell?'

Something inside her shrank. She said in a low voice, 'You know why, surely. You needed help and . . .'

'Not that kind of help,' he interrupted roughly. 'As well you knew, Courtney. He could have lent me the money—he knows he owes it to us. We're the injured parties in all this—something he seems to have lost sight of—and you're more than ready to overlook it too.'

She said, 'That's not true. Nothing can ever change what's happened. I know that only too well.'

She felt very close to tears. She had not expected Rob to be pleased at the news, or even grateful to her—she knew him too well for that—but she had not bargained for this attack.

He said, 'But that didn't stop you handing us over to him, lock, stock and barrel. Well, don't include me in your future plans. I shan't be joining the family circle at Hunters Court. And neither will your husband-to-be, very often, if all that Lynn Everett told me about his cosy little set-up with Miss Lydyard is true, but perhaps you don't mind the prospect of being humiliated.'

Courtney minded. She minded so much that it was like a physical agony consuming her, but she made no sign. After all, she'd had fair warning of the situation from Blair himself, although she hadn't realised at the time what he meant. No wonder he hadn't been disturbed at her insistence that she didn't want a real marriage! She remembered too his rather mocking remark about celibacy. It all fell so neatly into place.

Robin tossed the damp tea-towel on to the draining board with the muttered remark that he was going for a drink. Courtney tidied the kitchen slowly, then went into the living room, looking round her listlessly. The fire needed making up, the chair cushions were rumpled, and the paper which Rob had been scanning before the meal was lying on the floor in an untidy heap.

Courtney sank down on the rug in the middle of it all and put her hands over her face, letting the tears run down unchecked between her fingers. She'd cried little over the past three years. There'd been no time for emotionalism— she'd been too busy trying to drag some kind of life together out of the ruins. And now there was nothing but ruins again, and she was lost, lonely and afraid among them.

She cried until she had no more tears left, then she scrubbed her eyes with her fists fiercely and childishly, and looked up to see Blair standing staring at her.

She hadn't heard him come in. She'd been too absorbed in her private, painful world, and the shock drove all the colour from her face, leaving her icy pale with drowned eyes. She tried to struggle to her feet, and he was at her side immediately, his hand under her arm, helping her up. She shook him away almost savagely.

He stood back, the hazel eyes frankly speculative as they went over her. He said, 'Why were you crying?'

'What did you expect?' she flung at him fiercely. 'That I'd be dancing for joy?'

'I'm not as unrealistic as that,' he said coolly. 'Is it your father? He hasn't had another relapse?'

'Oh, no,' she said scornfully, 'he's doing very well. You'll be able to have your pound of flesh, whole and entire.'

And I'll bleed, she thought silently. I'll bleed to death.

'Good,' he said briefly. 'Then there must be some other explanation, unless you're going to plead female vapours.'

'I so plead,' she said. 'May we leave it at that?'

'Of course.' The tanned face was mocking. 'Now shall we go and have dinner?'

'I've already eaten, thanks.' She snatched up the newspaper and restored order to its pages, hoping the prosaic action would disguise the fact that she was trembling.

'Then you can come and watch me. You've got five minutes to bathe your eyes and do anything else you feel necessary.'

'Kindly don't give me orders!' she came back at him furiously. 'I'm not one of your downtrodden employees!'

'Is that how you think of them?' He sounded amused. 'I doubt if they'd agree with you. They're well paid, and I don't think I make excessive demands on them. None of them has ever hinted as much.'

'They'd be hardly likely to do that,' she said stonily. 'Have you brought Kate down this weekend?'

'No, she's spending it with her family. I do allow her some time to herself.' He was smiling now, but his eyes had narrowed slightly as though he was examining the association of ideas which had brought Kate's name into the conversation.

She could have kicked herself, but some demon drove her on.

'Have you told her that you've asked me to marry you?'

'I've told her that we're going to be married, yes,' he said rather drily, underlining the difference in emphasis in their words. 'Is it supposed to be a secret? Besides, Kate needed to know. She's doing the liaison work with the firm of decorators who'll be starting on the house next week.'

Courtney couldn't restrain a gasp. 'So soon?'

His brows went up. 'I see no reason for any further delay.'

Delay was hardly the word, she thought with a sense of mounting hysteria. Matters were proceeding with the speed of light!

She went upstairs and carried out more repairs to her face, applying blusher and eye-shadow with a light hand, then, on impulse, changed into a flowered cotton skirt with a matching quilted waistcoat, teaming them with a long-sleeved pink shirt which toned with the flowers. It was a favourite outfit from her rather limited wardrobe, and she felt buoyed up by it as she went downstairs.

The room had been tidied, she discovered, and the fire was burning comfortably again, with the spark guard already in place. Blair was standing by the hearth, his arm resting along the mantelshelf. His face looked sombre and a little tired, and Courtney wondered if he was thinking about all the inevitable problems and bitterness which would attend on this marriage between them.

She said, 'Blair,' and was amazed to hear how calm she sounded. 'Blair, it isn't too late. We don't have to go on with this farce. I'll repay you somehow if it takes the rest of my life, I swear I will—only don't make me do this thing. Don't make me marry you!'

He stared at her without moving, his face expressionless, but she could sense the anger in him—anger and something else.

At last he said sardonically, 'Skilful pleading, darling, but altogether too late, I'm afraid. I've waited too long for this, and there'll be no turning back for either of us. Now, shall we go?'

She assented in a low voice, and went to get her coat.

'No turning back.' The words seemed to drum in her brain with weary emphasis. And no way to halt what could only be a headlong race towards disaster.

CHAPTER SEVEN

SHE was relieved to find that Blair didn't intend to dine at the White Hart. She'd been afraid that he might, and that they'd run into Robin, because she wasn't sure she could stand another confrontation.

But instead he drove out of the village, and turned on to the main road.

'It's cold tonight,' he commented after a lengthy silence.

'It's been getting colder all this week,' she said. 'I think we may have some more snow.'

'Well, that deals fairly comprehensively with the weather,' he said. 'What shall we talk about next? The state of the economy? I imagine more personal topics are taboo.'

'No,' she said with something of an effort. 'Perhaps we should talk.'

'Bravo,' he approved softly. 'There's safety in words, Courtney. Silences tend towards intimacy, and we must avoid that at all costs.'

Courtney flinched from the edge in his words. 'I gave in my notice at work,' she said. 'Today was my last day. They—they've given us a wedding present.'

'How kind,' he said coolly. 'What was it?'

'Sheets, I think, and pillow cases. I haven't opened it yet.'

'And singularly inappropriate under the circumstances,' he said. 'But of course they weren't to know that. Unless you've had second thoughts.'

She sat rather straighter in her seat, which wasn't easy. 'No.'

'I didn't think so.' He sounded unperturbed.

This wasn't at all the kind of personal conversation she'd had in mind, and she cast around hurriedly for a change of subject.

'Robin says that you occupy very palatial offices. I was wondering what you did there?'

He said laconically, 'Ah yes, Robin. I was forgetting that he would have preceded me down here.' He was quiet for a moment, and she wondered uneasily whether he was making any connection between Rob's arrival and her tears earlier. But he made no comment. Instead he said, 'I trained as a surveyor, as I'm sure you know, but my chief interest was always in the mining and geological side. Basically, that's what it's all about—surveying possible sites for oil and minerals.'

Courtney said, 'Oh,' in a subdued manner, and he laughed. 'Well, what did you expect? A merchant bank like Carteret's, or dazzling dealings on the Stock Market? Not for me. Are you disappointed?'—with a lightning glance sideways at her.

She didn't know what to say. She was completely ignorant about the dealings of such a company as he had described, but while it might be successful, surely such a success had to be built up slowly and would need initial capital as well. So where had all the money come from?

At last she said woodenly, 'No, not disappointed. It—it sounds very interesting. Does it involve a lot of travelling?'

'Is that a tactful way of asking how much you'll be forced to see of me?' he asked derisively. 'Yes, darling, there can be a lot of travelling, depending rather on how deeply involved I choose to be. At the moment, I haven't quite decided about that. Bridegrooms aren't expected to rush round the world leaving their brides languishing at home alone. Or were you hoping for a honeymoon in Alaska or South America?'

'You know I wasn't,' she said tightly, staring down at her hands, clasped in her lap. 'I imagine we can do without a honeymoon.'

'Then think again,' he came back at her with a note of anger. 'Every convention is going to be observed, Courtney. Even that one. Somewhere in the world there has to be a hotel suite large enough to accommodate us both without damaging your outdated obsession with chastity.'

She remained silent, too mortified to speak, and after a moment he went on without any noticeable softening of his tone, 'Perhaps you'd make arrangements for us to see the Vicar next weekend. We need to have the banns called, and talk about the actual ceremony.'

'Banns?' she repeated sharply, unable to conceal her dismay. 'But I thought—a register office . . .'

'To hell with what you thought,' Blair said icily. 'Our wedding will take place at the village church in full view of any friends or enemies who take a fancy to be there. I have people to invite, as I'm sure you have, Courtney. There'll be no hole-and-corner affair. I'm going to call you my wife as publicly and as lavishly as I can.'

Her lips moved stiffly. 'All part of the rehabilitation process? Isn't a full village wedding carrying things a little too far?'

'Not for me. Anything else could be construed as a tacit admission on your part that you're ashamed of marrying me. While that may be the truth, it's a truth we'll keep confined to our immediate family circle.' He paused. 'Your father's still a sick man. Will Robin be prepared to give you away?'

'I don't know,' she said. 'You'd better ask him.'

'In other words, he could refuse. Well, that figures,' said Blair. 'Would you object to Philip Carteret instead?'

'No,' she said rather helplessly. 'But he might not . . .'

'Take my word for it that he will. Can I construe from a note in your voice earlier that you won't be asking Kate to be your bridesmaid?'

'Yes,' she said, much too quickly; and was thankful that the dimness inside the car hid the sudden flush in her cheeks.

'As you please,' he said with utter indifference, and said no more until they arrived at their destination.

It was another inn, even older than the White Hart, and situated by the river, which the dining room windows overlooked. One glance at the menu made

Courtney sadly regret the cottage pie, and it didn't take a great deal of persuasion to convince her that she could manage at least a lobster cocktail, served in an exotically rich sauce, and one of the delectable sweets on the trolley. *Millefeuilles*, she thought with frank greed, or profiteroles.

As for Blair, it would be stretching a point to say that he set out to be charming, but at least he seemed to want to put her at her ease, and any further mention of the wedding was avoided, to her relief.

Here she was, supping with the devil yet again, Courtney thought with a little inward sigh. Her analogy had been more appropriate than she could ever have dreamed, because surely the marriage he was forcing her into would be the very worst kind of hell . . .

The drive home was uneventful. Blair put a Sky tape on the stereo, and she relaxed, glad to listen to the music. She knew so little about him, she thought, or at least none of the details that any engaged girl might be expected to know—his preferences in food, for instance, or his taste in music. She didn't know what films he'd seen, if any, or if he ever went to the theatre. And the thought that she had the rest of her life to discover such things brought no comfort at all.

She had hoped that Blair would simply drop her at the cottage as it was late when they got back, but it was soon clear that he had no such intention. He locked the car and accompanied her to the front door, and when, rather reluctantly, she produced her key, he took it from her, fitted it in the door, then stood aside to allow her to precede him into the living room.

There was no sign of Robin, but as it was long past closing time he could well have returned and gone straight up to bed, Courtney thought.

Feeling oddly tonguetied, she said, 'The fire's nearly out.'

'It can be revived.' Blair sounded amused. 'I'll see to it while you make us some coffee.'

She nodded unwillingly and went towards the kitchen, wishing that she'd bade him a firm goodnight on the doorstep. It had always worked perfectly well with Clive, she thought, but she had an uneasy feeling that Blair would not have accepted his dismissal quite so easily.

The fire was burning cheerfully when she returned with the tray, and Blair was lounging on the sofa watching the leaping flames through half-closed eyes, his jacket discarded and his tie loosened.

Courtney's heart sank as she set down the tray. Bathed by lamplight and the flickering flames, the room seemed to enclose them in a small, intimate world, and this was the last thing she wanted. She took care to choose a seat by the fire, leaving Blair to occupy the sofa alone.

The lines of his face were set in weariness and the hazel eyes were meditative and abstracted. Courtney watched him under her lashes, pretending to be concentrating on her coffee. It occurred to her, sinkingly, that this would only be the first of many such evenings when she would sit, giving him covert glances, trying desperately to think of something sufficiently impersonal as a topic of conversation. She suppressed a little sigh, feeling the now familiar pain strike deep within her.

She leaned forward to put her empty cup down on the hearth, and as she did so, she noticed that Blair was looking at her. She met his gaze, feeling her heart begin to thud, and it was suddenly necessary to fill the silence with words.

She said hurriedly, 'I haven't thanked you yet—for what you've done for Robin. It—it must have been very unpleasant for you. What did he say—when you gave him the money?'

The firm lips quirked at the corners. 'He said nothing to me. It was all carried out between our lawyers. What did you imagine—that we met at midnight in the corner of a bombed-out warehouse like some bad movie on television?'

She flushed. 'I suppose—something like that. Is that the end of it, then? There'll be no—no . . .'

'No comebacks?' he supplied. 'No, you don't have to worry about that, Courtney. You've seen the last of Montague Pallister, if that's what you want to hear.'

'Yes,' she said, with an involuntary shiver. She hesitated for a moment. 'I hope that Rob thanked you too.'

Blair's smile mocked her. 'Now that would be too much to ask! Coming to his rescue was both my pleasure and my privilege, or so I was led to infer.'

Courtney's flush deepened. 'I'm sorry,' she said in a mortified tone.

'Don't be. I've known Rob for a long time. I didn't really expect anything else, particularly once he'd found out that we were going to be married.'

And that wasn't all he found out, Courtney thought painfully. She wanted to ask him about Kate—about the flat. But it was impossible. She had no right. The terms between them had been agreed, and she couldn't vary them now by behaving like a jealous fiancée. For her pride's sake, it was much better to pretend total ignorance of the situation.

She said flatly, 'That hasn't pleased him at all.'

'Pleasing your brother isn't the objective I have in mind.' His own rejoinder was equally unemotional, but his glance sharpened. 'What's he been saying to you, Courtney?'

'Nothing,' she denied hurriedly.

'Little liar. You can carry family loyalty too far, you know.'

'You're the last person who should level that particular criticism,' she said unsteadily. 'Aren't you doing precisely that? Isn't that why you're pushing me into this—farcical marriage?'

She got to her feet as she spoke and Blair rose too.

'I'm sorry you regard it as a farce,' he said coolly. 'Perhaps I should make it clear that I'm in deadly earnest about it, whatever your private feelings may be—and I suspect you're not even sure about them. But there's one good way of finding out.'

By the time she'd read the purpose in his face as he

moved towards her, escape was out of the question. The fireplace was behind her, and to reach the door she had to get past Blair.

She said falteringly in a voice she barely recognised as her own, 'Oh no—please, no!' but it was no use. His hands were already descending on her shoulders, drawing her towards him quite inexorably, and then his mouth was on hers, warm and urgently sensuous, compelling the response she was no longer capable of withholding.

Her lips parted, welcoming the deeper intimacy he was demanding. His hand cradled the nape of her neck, his thumb moving softly and rhythmically against the sensitive hollow beneath her ear while the kiss went on endlessly, sending her dizzyingly into realms of sensation she had never dreamed existed.

But dreams no longer mattered. Now there was only reality—the utter reality of Blair's body, hard and strong against hers, the possessive slide of his hand as he moulded her to him, the warmth of his skin as she clutched almost helplessly at his shirt, trying vainly to steady herself on legs which no longer seemed capable of supporting her.

His arms tightened around her, lifting her totally into his embrace, and he was moving, sinking down on the rug in front of the fireplace, lowering her gently on to its softness, his mouth leaving hers at last to explore the line of her throat with little kisses, gentle as the brush of silk on her skin.

She sighed with pleasure, her body arching towards his in mute invitation, the last vestiges of control slipping away as his mouth continued its warm insidious downward path. The buttons on her shirt had not even offered a token difficulty, and nor had the little clip which fastened her bra between her breasts, she realised dazedly.

His lean fingers encompassed the soft roundness they had so effortlessly uncovered, coaxing the delicate peaks into a small agony of pleasure which brought a smothered moan from her. Then his mouth was on her, the sensual tug of his lips making her slender body twist mindlessly in delight, his tongue teasing as a feather on her heated flesh. She lifted languid fingers, tangling them in his hair, cradling his head against her. Every nerve in her body seemed linked to some great primeval pulse, and its beat was like thunder in her ears, so loud that she thought Blair must hear it too.

When at last he lifted his head and looked at her, the hazel eyes were brilliant with desire. He said huskily, 'Sweet—darling, you're so sweet. I'm going to kiss every perfect inch of you . . .'

It wouldn't stop at kissing, she thought. It couldn't. This flame of wanting him was burning her up. He had discarded his shirt and his skin was golden in the firelight. As his mouth found hers, she wound her arms around him, discovering joyously the play of muscle under the smooth skin of his back.

With a sound between a laugh and a groan, Blair murmured her name against her lips, and his hand slid down to the waistband of her skirt. She made no resistance, her body pliant and responsive as he lifted her slightly to free her from the clinging folds of material, but she was trembling a little, and he paused, looking down at her, his brows raised questioningly.

She said, 'Blair—I've never . . .'

He brushed a finger across her lips, silencing her. 'Do you think I don't know that? There's nothing to be afraid of, sweetheart, I swear it.' He kissed her, his mouth lingering on hers, his hands moving gently and smoothly until, almost without being aware of it, she was naked in his arms.

Blair said softly, 'You're lovely. Courtney, I . . . ' He paused suddenly, lifting himself away from her, his gaze turning towards the stairs and the half-closed door which led to them.

Enclosed in her shimmering sphere of desire and arousal, Courtney hadn't heard the footsteps coming down the stairs. It was the door being flung back on its hinges which brought her to swift, startled realisation of the fact that they weren't alone any more. Blair moved sharply, interposing himself between her and the door. Over his bare shoulder she saw Robin, astonishment and a kind of appalled horror giving way to rage on his face. Flinching, she heard him swear obscenely at them both before turning and retreating back upstairs, stumbling as he went.

Blair swore too, coldly and fluently as he leapt to his feet, and went after him.

Shaking violently, Courtney dragged herself on to her knees. If she had burned before, she was now icy cold. Moving like an automaton, she reached for her clothes, pulling them on with fingers that were hardly able to cope with buttons and zips. When she had finished, she sat with her knees drawn up to her chin, her face buried in her folded arms.

At last she heard Blair coming back. Shuddering, she closed her eyes so tightly that bright glittering sparks danced behind her eyelids. But he didn't speak or attempt to touch her, and the sound of his movements told her that he was dressing too.

Eventually, she lifted her head and looked at him. He was standing leaning one arm on the mantelpiece, regarding the knuckles of his right hand with a faintly rueful air.

She said hoarsely, 'What have you done to him?'

His mouth curled. 'He's still alive. A split lip, nothing more.'

Her voice choked. 'How horrible!'

His glance was caustic. 'You're used to hearing that kind of language from him, then?'

She shook her head. 'No—of course not. But he—he didn't realise what he was saying. He was shaken . . .'

'Really?' The lift of his brows was totally cynical. 'I'd never thought Robin was so sensitive. It's fortunate, then, that he arrived when he did, and not five minutes later.'

'No.' Her face flaming, Courtney moved her head in violent negation.

'Oh, yes,' he said softly. 'Don't bother to deny it, darling, because you're fooling no one but yourself.

You were ready and much more than willing, and you know it.' He came away from the mantelpiece with a kind of controlled violence, and she shrank.

'Don't touch me!'

He laughed savagely. 'Back into your shell, Courtney? Well, don't rely on its protection in future, my sweet, not now you've shown me how easily it can be cracked.'

She swallowed. 'I—I feel dirty.'

His mouth compressed itself thinly. 'Any dirt exists only in your mind, darling, nowhere else. Everything I wanted, you wanted too. If Robin hadn't come blundering in when he did, we'd have been lovers now.'

Courtney said thickly, 'Then I'm thankful that he did "blunder in". Otherwise I'd feel totally degraded.'

Blair said very quietly, 'You're unbelievable, Courtney. Do you know that? Only minutes ago you were a warm, loving woman, everything a man could want in his arms. Now you're a sulky little spitfire. I'm going to pretend I didn't hear your last remark, otherwise I might be tempted to put you across my knee and give you the hiding you so richly deserve.'

He reached for his jacket, and shrugged it on. 'I'll see you tomorrow,' he added flatly, and left.

For a long time, Courtney sat where she was, staring into the embers of the fire. Even if her mind shrank wincing from what Blair had said to her, she knew it was no more than the truth. But for Robin, his conquest of her would have been complete. She might not have said the words, 'I love you', but her body in its uninhibited response to his kisses and caresses had betrayed her a dozen times.

At last, she got up stiffly and went upstairs. She paused outside Robin's room, and said his name in a low voice, but there was no response of any kind, and defeatedly Courtney went into her own room and shut the door.

She slept badly, and did not wake until well past her usual time. She dressed and went downstairs with some reluctance, dreading the inevitable confrontation with Robin, but he wasn't there, although the kitchen bore signs of a hasty breakfast not cleared away. Sighing, Courtney piled the used dishes into the sink, and then paused, noticing that his car had gone from the yard. She turned off the taps and went up to his room. The door was closed still, but she knew almost resignedly what she would find when she opened it. The place was bare except for the unmade bed, wardrobe doors yawning open and empty drawers pulled out haphazardly.

He had gone, and without a word.

Feeling slightly sick, Courtney stripped the bed, and put the room straight. Robin's behaviour over the past twelve hours had delivered one shock after another, but this was the worst, and she felt hurt and bewildered. Presumably Robin had deserted her because he had decided she was now on the side of the enemy.

She wandered over to the window and stood looking out with unseeing eyes. After what he had witnessed the night before, she supposed she could understand his point of view. If she'd only been able to see him, talk to him, she might have been able to convince him that she was torn—desperately torn between her feelings for Blair, and her loyalty to her family.

She could have reminded him too that he himself had urged an approach to Blair to help him out of his difficulties. She gave a little stifled sigh. She could say all kinds of things, embark on all kinds of recriminations, but what good would it do? It wouldn't change anything, wouldn't release her from this trap she was in.

Not to her surprise, Blair was waiting for her when she arrived back downstairs. He was standing by the table, glancing rather impatiently through the paper, but he tossed it aside as she came in, and gave her a long look. His brows drew together in a swift frown.

'What is it?' he demanded. He put a hand under her chin, tilting her face towards him so that he could study it more closely.

'Leave me alone!' Fiercely she jerked herself away from his touch.

A wintry smile touched his lips. 'So you've decided to

revive your one-woman resistance movement? Well, play whatever little game seems best to you, sweetheart, because that's all it is, we both know it.' He paused. 'How's Rob this morning?'

'I don't know.'

'Still sulking in his room?'

Courtney shook her head, aware of a sudden lump in her throat. 'No.' She swallowed. 'As a matter of fact, I don't know where he's gone.'

'I see,' he said, after a moment. 'And naturally you blame me.'

'Not entirely.' She made herself speak steadily. 'I suppose it was—inevitable.'

'Yes, I think it was,' Blair agreed. 'Since I bailed him out with friend Pallister, your brother must have been finding it increasingly difficult to live with himself.'

'That isn't altogether what I meant,' she said.

'I'm sure it isn't.' He eyed her with faint mockery. 'Well, what do you want? Rob brought back?'

She shook her head. 'He's made his choice, and I can't blame him. I—I can't make him accept the situation.' She hesitated, then said stiffly, 'Please, Blair, don't force him to come back. It—it wouldn't work.'

'I've no such intention,' he said drily. 'He'll come back in his own good time anyway. I guarantee it.' There was an odd note in his voice, but Courtney was too depressed and weary to question it.

Later they drove to Wolverton. In the market square there was a small branch of a famous London jeweller, and Courtney discovered that Blair had ordered a selection of engagement and wedding rings to be sent down especially for her to choose from. Courtney looked down at the trays of sparkling stones proffered for her inspection and had to fight back tears. Standing with the man she loved, choosing together the ring which would be the outward symbol of that love— wasn't that every girl's dream? If Blair loved her, if they had been marrying for the right reasons, then this should have been a magic moment in their relationship. As it was . . .

Obediently she tried on rings, held out her hand to see the effect, heard Blair call her 'darling', and the manager's deferential murmur as he chose yet another exquisite gem for her to try.

She heard her own voice, bright and brittle. 'They're all so beautiful, darling. You choose for me.'

The expression in the hazel eyes was frankly cynical as Blair picked clearly the most expensive ring in the collection—a diamond solitaire perfectly cut and mounted, and glowing with a deep inner fire. At least Courtney guessed it was the most expensive. Nothing as sordid as money had been mentioned during the entire transaction. The ring fitted too, so there was no excuse not to wear it.

She saw the expression on the girl assistant's face, a mixture of sentiment and envy, and thought, 'If you knew . . . if you only knew . . .'

Blair took her hand as they left the shop, and the clasp of his lean fingers round hers sent a shaft of unwitting, uncontrollable excitement through her body. She bit her lip as they walked back to the car. If a casual touch could have such an effect on her, what hope was there if he decided to launch the same kind of onslaught on her senses as he had the previous night?

But as the weekend wore on, it seemed that Blair had no such intention. They spent several hours at Hunters Court looking at patterns of wallpapers and fabrics. In the evening he took her out to dinner, but afterwards, having seen her into the cottage presumably to assure himself that everything was as it should be, he left almost at once, saying abruptly that she looked tired. On Sunday he drove her to Wolverton to see her father, but he made no attempt to share the visit. He sat in the car outside with the papers while Courtney went in alone. After, he drove her home, but left almost at once, apparently to return to London.

Alone, Courtney felt confused and uncertain, as if she was living in a dream. But on her hand Blair's diamond glittered, its cold fire an all too potent reminder of the bitterness of reality.

She still felt confused, barely a month later when she stood in the vast bedroom at Hunters Court, slender in her cream silk going-away outfit. Unwillingly she looked at herself in the full-length mirror. Anna, her bridesmaid, who had trained as a beautician after leaving school, had made her up expertly for her wedding, but cosmetics couldn't disguise the too-defined line of her cheekbones, or the expression of frightened desperation in her eyes.

It had been no more than the truth when she had reflected on the speed at which things were happening. But in the past weeks, even that devastating momentum had increased, until here she was—a married woman. Blair Devereux's wife.

Anna had helped her change out of her lace and chiffon wedding dress, but Courtney had urged her to return to the reception downstairs, and Anna had been far from reluctant to do so. She was getting on incredibly well with the best man, she had told Courtney candidly.

Courtney wasn't altogether surprised. Grant Westcott was a tall, good-looking Texan with clear blue eyes and a slow smile, whom Blair had described briefly as a friend. Courtney found herself wondering how they had met, and where and when, but none of that information seemed to be forthcoming, from either of them. Grant made her laugh, and paid her extravagant compliments, but he adroitly sidestepped even the most delicately phrased questions.

As for Blair, the past three years might as well have taken place in a vacuum. He never referred to them at all.

She shivered slightly, tugging at the neckline of her jacket with nervous fingers. These minutes alone would provide her with a brief respite, but all too soon she would have to go downstairs and face everyone again.

The ceremony had been the ordeal she had anticipated. The church had been full, but Courtney suspected that at least half the guests were there from curiosity, not because they wished them well particularly. She had been conscious all the time of the speculation in the glances directed at her as she walked up the aisle on Philip Carteret's arm. She had heard nothing from Rob since he'd walked out of the cottage, and had received neither a present or any kind of greeting from him to mark the wedding. But that, she supposed, would have been too much to hope.

However, her father had been there, in a wheelchair still, admittedly, and she knew his presence had been a satisfaction to Blair, and a talking point for everyone else. He had kissed Courtney and told her how beautiful she looked, and shaken hands with his son-in-law as if their marriage was everything he'd always hoped and planned for. By this time, too, word had got round that when Blair and Courtney returned from their honeymoon in the Caribbean, he would be moving back to Hunters Court to live with them, and she knew that all kinds of questions were being asked by everyone who remembered the three-year-old scandal.

Courtney gave a brief sigh as she looked around her. It was amazing how quickly and how well things could be done when money was no object. The room was barely recognisable now, the faintly shabby furnishings swept away. A Chinese carpet in shades of turquoise and apple blossom covered the floor, and these colours were picked up in the quilted cover on the enormous bed, and the floor-length curtains at the windows. This room, and the dressing room and bathroom which opened from it, had been the first to be completed, and she could remember only too well standing here, gazing round, registering that bed and all it implied, and unable to protest, to even say a word because Kate was there too. She remembered Blair's eyes, mocking her, daring her to speak.

In the end, she said, 'It's beautiful,' in a colourless voice, and turned away.

There was in fact a single bed in the dressing room, but she had no guarantee that Blair would use it. The subject had simply never been discussed, and she was loath to reintroduce it—especially as Blair had hardly touched or kissed her since their engagement.

She was forced to admit to a faint bewilderment. Usually he brushed his lips across her cheek in greeting or farewell, but there was no sign of the hungry passion he had shown her that night at the cottage. In fact sometimes she wondered if she had dreamed that whole disturbing episode, yet surely a dream, would not have left as its legacy the aching physical awareness that invaded her whenever she was near him.

Of course, it was true to say they had hardly been alone together in the past month. The rush of arrangements for the wedding had taken up a lot of time, and she had spent ten days in London staying with the Carterets at their invitation while she shopped for clothes.

She had expected Blair would invite her to his offices, but he had not done so, and Courtney had not asked, wondering if perhaps he didn't want Kate to know she was in London.

She had been frankly dreading meeting the other girl again, and was thankful at their next encounter at Hunters Court that the decorators were there, and one of the interior designers. Kate had wished her happiness, smilingly, but her blue eyes were like stones. Courtney found herself wondering whether Kate had let herself believe that Blair was buying Hunters Court for her, convincing herself that from lover to wife was only a short step which she could easily negotiate.

If so, even in her own unhappiness she could find compassion for her, if not liking. She would never regain any of the old schoolday camaraderie, she knew. There was too much between them. As it was, when Blair was at the house she found she was watching them together almost compulsively, looking for the smallest sign of intimacy, the least clue that their relationship still continued.

In Kate's place, Courtney thought fiercely, she would not have stayed. She would have resigned instantly and gone away somewhere. But then she did not know what had been said between them, what explanation Blair had given her for his marriage. Perhaps Kate knew that any relationship established on such shaky foundations could not last, and she was content to play a waiting game.

The thought made Courtney feel slightly sick, and she tried to avoid visiting the house when she knew Kate and be there. She suspected Kate was aware of this even even amused by it, even though the courteous civility she extended to Courtney as her employer's fiancée never wavered.

But in the last week Mrs Garvin had taken over, and Courtney was free to come and go as she pleased. She had liked Mrs Garvin instantly. She was a stoutly built middle-aged woman, efficient and capable without being a martinet, whom nothing ever seemed to fluster. Dealing with florists, caterers and palpably nervous brides was clearly all in a day's work to her, Courtney realised with faint amusement.

The only point of contention so far had been over her father's room. Courtney had discovered that one of the first floor rooms was being prepared, and had protested, saying that the ground floor would cause him less problems. But Mrs Garvin had been unexpectedly firm, telling her that Mr Devereux had been quite specific about the room and its siting. Puzzled, Courtney had taken the matter up with Blair at once, but it had made no difference.

He had given her a cool look. 'A ground floor room? Isn't that emphasising the fact that he's an invalid— more helpless than he actually is? I don't think he'd thank you for that, Courtney. Let's leave the arrangements as they are, for the time being at least.'

She stared at him. 'All this consideration for a man you don't even like,' she said rather shakily. 'Are you sure it's that, Blair, or do you just want to keep him a prisoner upstairs?'

'What a melodramatic imagination you have, sweetheart,' he drawled. 'I promise you I've no such intention. And I think you'll be surprised to find how well your father can manage the stairs,' he added with a faint smile.

'As you wish,' she said shortly, with a shrug.

'Yes,' he said, the hazel eyes suddenly hard and brooding. 'That's it exactly, Courtney. Everything just as I wish.'

Courtney shivered slightly, remembering. There had been an unmistakable note of warning in his voice, but she had no need of it, she thought bitterly. She was only too well aware of the problems confronting her.

A knock at the bedroom door startled her, shattering her reverie. It wouldn't be Blair, she thought. He wouldn't tap politely and wait to be granted admittance. This was his house now, and everything in it belonged to him, herself included, and she still had no idea how far he was prepared to carry that possession.

She forced herself to sound cool and composed. 'Come in.'

The door opened and Kate Lydyard walked into the room. Courtney stared at her, frankly taken aback. Apart from a brief moment in the receiving line when she had wished them well, Kate had kept well in the background at the reception.

She said now with a smile that did not reach her eyes, 'You've been gone rather a long time. If you don't come down soon Blair will think you've run away.'

Courtney turned away on the pretext of searching for her bag. 'I hardly think so. After all——' she lifted her shoulders in a shrug, 'where could I run to—and why?'

'Why indeed?' Kate agreed mockingly. 'Just when everything you've ever wanted has been handed to you on a plate.' Her smile had become fixed and sharp, and her breathing had quickened. 'So you thought better of making him wait for ever. That's very wise of you, Courtney. Blair can be quite ruthless about getting what he wants. He won't stand for any opposition either, but no doubt you've discovered that for yourself by now.'

'Yes,' said Courtney. 'But thanks for the friendly

warning just the same.' Her tone was deliberately ironic.

'If that's how you want to interpret it.' The blue eyes were inimical and cold. They swept past Courtney and round the room resting briefly on the filmy white folds of the wedding dress discarded across the bed before returning to Courtney, slender in her cream silk dress with its matching long-sleeved jacket.

'Very virginal,' she commented lightly. 'But are you sure that's what he wants.'

Courtney looked steadily back. 'Another warning?' she queried, but her heart thudded as she found herself wondering just how much of Blair's confidence Kate enjoyed. It made her skin crawl to think the other girl might know of the desperate panic-stricken little bargain she had tried to make with him, perhaps even laughed about it with him. She picked up her bag and started for the door.

'I wouldn't like you to have any unrealistic ideas about this marriage of yours,' Kate said venomously. 'You're being married for expediency—for no other reason. You were always a child, Courtney, and Blair needs a woman. Never forget that.'

For a moment she was afraid that Kate was going to come after her. That they were going to walk down the stairs together in a hideous semblance of amity, but at least she was spared that. She was alone when she reached the hall, and the laughing, chattering crowd of people waiting to see her leave with Blair on their honeymoon.

He had changed too from the formality of morning dress into a pale grey suit with a silky texture. He moved to the foot of the stairs to meet her, taking her hand and raising it to his lips with a kind of careless charm while everyone cheered.

Anna looking flushed and sparkling edged towards them. 'Where's your bouquet?' she hissed. 'You're supposed to throw it . . .'

'Oh, heavens!' Courtney faltered for a moment. 'I'd forgotten. I've left it upstairs.'

She half-turned, but Blair stopped her, his hand adamantly drawing hers through his arm. 'That's one superstition we'll have to forgo,' he said. 'You can't retreat back to your sanctuary again, darling. We have a plane to catch.' He was smiling, but his eyes were watchful as they rested on her.

She was thankful to find herself outside in the car. She made herself wave and smile her goodbyes, and all the time she knew if she looked up at the first floor she would see Kate watching her, hating her, envying her . . .

She swallowed convulsively, thankful for the warmth of the mink jacket Blair had put solicitously round her shoulders, before they went out into the bleak wind. Another unexpected, expensive gift, for which she had barely uttered a shy word of thanks. She'd seen the derisive, slanting smile on his lips as they descended the terrace steps, and a little coil of nervousness tightened inside her.

She glanced back over her shoulder, but the house had disappeared, hidden by the sweeping curve of the drive.

Blair said, 'Alone at last.' But the lightness of his tone was belied by the suddenly searching glance he sent her.

Courtney's face flamed, and her hand clenched round her bag as she muttered, 'Yes.'

She expected him to say something else, but he remained silent. Nor did he make any further attempt to move the conversation on to a personal level. The few remarks they exchanged on the long drive to the airport concerned the weather and road conditions, and occasionally he enquired if she was warm enough or if she wanted to stop for some kind of refreshment.

She slept on the plane, although she hadn't expected to do so. When they landed in warm alien darkness, she felt disorientated, and she stood almost submissively while Blair dealt swiftly and efficiently with all the tiresome details of their arrival. As they left the airport in a chauffeur-driven hired car, it occurred to her that she hadn't the faintest idea where they were bound for.

It wasn't a hotel, she soon discovered. It was a house—a large rambling villa furnished with a kind of casual luxury, and standing in its own grounds which led down to a private beach. From the balcony of her room she could hear the whisper of the sea. She turned and went back into the lamplit room. Her luggage was there, waiting. Blair had told her not to bother about changing. Missie, one of the servants, would unpack for her while they were having dinner, he had said, before he had gone into the adjoining bedroom and closed the door.

Courtney did some swift repairs to her make-up and hair and went downstairs, where Bertram and Lena, the couple who looked after the house, were waiting. Their faces were beaming with pride and pleasure as they showed her into the big ground-floor living room where Blair was waiting, drink in hand. The room was on two levels, the dining area being approached by two shallow steps. Courtney had little appetite, but she had to admit that the platters of seafood accompanied by exotic salads looked appealing, and she saw that there was champagne waiting on ice. All the ingredients for a romantic wedding night supper, she thought ironically, except that Blair was treating her as prosaically as if they'd been married for a dozen years or more. She supposed she ought to feel grateful, but her overriding emotion was one of uncertainty.

Looking round, she noticed that Bertram and Lena had tactfully vanished, and she flushed slightly as Blair bent towards her, refilling her glass.

'Do—do the servants live in?' she asked.

'They have their own cottage in the grounds,' he said. 'Missie is Lena's younger sister.'

'Oh,' she digested this, wondering how he knew so much about the domestic situation. 'I didn't know you could hire houses like this. It's very large.'

'Wasn't that what you wanted?' The hazel eyes were

suddenly cool and direct, and her flush deepened as she remembered that other earlier exchange.

'It's a beautiful house,' she prevaricated, taking a hasty sip of champagne. 'And they've made us so welcome.'

Blair sent her a sardonic look. 'As they're paid to do,' he reminded her.

'I suppose so,' she said slowly, feeling put down. 'But that doesn't always make a great deal of difference to people's attitudes. Bertram and Lena behave as if they're genuinely glad to have us here, and yet I suppose we're only one of a series of couples. I imagine this is the sort of place that would be used a lot for honeymoons.'

His brows lifted. 'What makes you think that?'

'Well——' Courtney was suddenly aware that she had strayed into deep waters, 'it—it's very private, isn't it—and romantic too,' she ended on a little rush, looking down at her plate.

'It is indeed,' he agreed mockingly. 'Perhaps in the circumstances we should have gone elsewhere.'

The man who had held and caressed her with such tender passion might never have existed. He bore no relation at all to the cynically smiling stranger at the other end of the dining table.

'Don't look so shattered.' His voice roughened slightly. 'We're here and we're staying. Do I infer that in spite of your girlish enthusiasm for privacy and romance, you still wish to adhere to the terms of our previous agreement?'

No, she thought despairingly. No, I don't. I want you to come round the table to me, and take me in your arms and love me, and make everything right.

She wasn't capable of saying the words, but she knew that all she need do was look at him and smile, and that would be enough. Because however coolly he phrased his query, he wanted her. She knew he did, and that was why she never moved or looked at him. Because she didn't want the emptiness of lovemaking without love. Physical pleasure however intense could never be enough. She wanted his heart and soul too, and she would never have them because there was too much between them.

After a long time Blair said drily, 'In some contexts silence means consent, but not, I think, with you, Courtney.'

'No,' she acknowledged unhappily, still not looking at him.

He uttered a harsh sound between a laugh and a sigh. 'Then I suggest you go to bed. You've had a long day.' He paused, then said with irony, 'Take the champagne with you, if you want.'

'No, thanks.' Courtney pushed back the chair and stood up, her face pale and unhappy. 'I—I'm sorry.'

He lifted his glass towards her in a mocking toast. 'So am I—would you believe.'

On a whisper, she said, 'You should have married Kate. Why didn't you?'

'Because that wasn't part of the plan,' he said cruelly. 'What do you want me to say next? A virtuous denial that there's ever been anything between us?'

'Would it be true?' His words seemed to stab her like knives, but she concealed it.

'Why should you care?' he asked wearily. 'All in all, Courtney, things are probably better as they are. We'll keep our sterile bargain, darling, until it outlives its usefulness. Now go to bed, before I change my mind.'

The sudden note of savagery in his voice was all that Courtney needed, and she fled.

In her room, she stripped and showered and put on a lace nightgown. Then she climbed into bed and switched off the big lamp, then lay watching the narrow line of light coming under the door from the adjoining room, and wondering what she would do, what she would say if, in spite of everything, the door began to open.

A long time later she heard Blair come up. Her body taut as a bowstring, she lay and listened to him moving about, watching the door, waiting, almost hoping. Then the light snapped off, and everything went quiet.

And Courtney was there, alone, in the silence and the darkness.

CHAPTER EIGHT

THE days passed somehow. One seemed to meld into another with the sun, and the white sands of the beach and the soft roll and hiss of the waves.

Courtney sunbathed a lot, cautiously at first, using plenty of sun-screen, and then with more abandon as her body began to tan beautifully and evenly. Blair rarely joined her, although he normally came to the beach to swim each day before lunch. He'd brought a briefcase of work with him, and seemed to spend a major part of each day on the telephone, in spite of the vagaries of the local exchange which she heard him discussing blasphemously with Bertram more than once.

Courtney had felt selfconscious at first, aware that Bertram and his wife knew that she and Blair were on honeymoon, and yet occupying separate rooms, but neither of them nor Missie gave the slightest hint that they found the situation in any way unusual. Perhaps they assumed Blair visited her, then went back to his own room to sleep, she thought.

But they were wrong. The door between their rooms remained as firmly shut as it had done that first night. And she had long since given up lying in the darkness waiting for the strip of light under the door to fade, because sometimes Blair didn't come to his room until the early hours of the morning.

Gradually, as the pattern of their days became more established, Courtney became more daring about her sunbathing, eventually discarding the top of her bikini altogether during the hours when she could be sure of having the beach to herself. At first she was on edge, unable to relax completely because she was always watching the path which led between a tangle of exotically flowering shrubs back to the house, and

145

listening for Blair's approach. But the daily assurance
of her privacy eased her tension at last.

Sometimes she swam with him, revelling in the warm
and relatively tranquil waters of the lagoon. At first she
had been reluctant, anxious to avoid even such a
minimal amount of intimacy, but Blair seemed as keen
to keep their relationship on a totally casual footing as
she was. She had never done any skin-diving, but she
discovered its pleasures under his tutelage. A couple of
times Blair hired a boat and went fishing. Courtney
didn't want to take part herself, but she went along
anyway, knowing that as all Blair's attention would be
concentrated on what he was doing, she could feast her
eyes on him to her heart's content. It was safe then as it
never was at the house to sit and adore him with her
eyes, to let herself look with open desire at the lean
brown body, watch the play of muscles under the
supple skin.

Once, to her horror, she had found she was being
watched in turn, by Lysander, the boat's skipper, and
one of Bertram's many cousins on the island. She had
felt hideously embarrassed, but his white teeth had
flashed in a broad grin of such understanding and
approval that the awkward moment had passed. But
then Lysander obviously considered that she was a
happy bride stealing loving glances at the creator of
that happiness. She wondered cynically what his
expression would be if he knew the truth.

They were nearing the end of the second week of
their stay when Courtney fell asleep on the beach. She
had dozed before, lulled by the sound of the sea, and
the rustle of the breeze in the palm trees which fringed
the sand, but always some inner warning system had
been active, reminding her not to sleep too long.

This time it failed. She didn't know what woke her
eventually, but she opened her eyes dazedly to see Blair
standing over her, his shadow falling over her half
naked body. He was very still, as if he'd been moulded
out of granite, and the dark glasses he was wearing gave
him an enigmatic and almost sinister look.

Courtney sat up with a gasp. Her bikini top was lying beside her, but it was too late to start fumbling with that now. In a gesture as old as time, her hands went up to cover her breasts. He moved then, dropping down on one knee beside her, his mouth twisting sardonically.

'Why hide?' he asked. 'I've an excellent memory. And if you want an all-over tan, why not get one?' His hand went to the curve of her hip, tugging loose the flimsy bow which fastened her briefs.

She said on a shaken breath, 'No—no!'

'Why not?' His voice slowed to a drawl, the little scar on his cheekbone looking furiously white. 'I promised I wouldn't touch, but I said nothing about looking.'

On a little cracked note, Courtney said, 'But—you are—touching.'

His voice was almost grim. 'So—I cheat. What are you going to do about it?'

Not a thing, she thought, her mouth dry with sudden excitement. As he bent over her, his head and shoulders blotted out the sun, and she closed her eyes, her lips parting ecstatically as his mouth founds hers. Her hands went up, locking behind his head, her fingers fastening in his hair as she held him to her.

His lips moved languidly down the line of her throat to her shoulders and lower, and she shivered with delight as his tongue made tender magic around the aroused peaks of her breasts. She was dissolving in pleasure as his hands moved on her, wickedly expert, bringing her slowly but very surely to the point where no return was possible.

She was whispering his name as if it was an invocation, her own hands feverish as they stroked his sun-warmed flesh.

Blair groaned, 'Darling—yes, oh yes . . .' His voice thickened, and he began to kiss her again, his own control, she realised, stretched almost to breaking point.

Each day, she had attuned her senses to warn her when anyone approached down the path, but now, as the warning signals started to go off in her brain, she didn't believe it. Blair was here in her arms, so how could it be true?

She started to say hoarsely, 'Someone—on the path . . .' but Blair was already rolling away from her, cursing under his breath as he reached with the speed of light for the towel he had brought and draped it across her body.

Bertram appeared, grinning cheerfully. 'Visitors, Mister Blair,' he announced. 'Mister and Missus Hamilton. I tol' them you were on honeymoon, but they jus' won't take no for an answer.'

'I can believe that,' Blair said resignedly. 'Tell them I'll be right with them, Bertram.'

When Bertram had vanished, Blair bent and kissed Courtney, his mouth gentle, frank compunction in his eyes. 'Sweet, I'm sorry, but I know Jeff and Abby of old. They're the persistent types.'

'You know them?' She shook her head bewilderedly. 'Then you've been here before?'

He hesitated, then nodded. 'Yes. I'd better go up to the house, before they come looking for us. Will you join us when you're ready? I'll have to ask them to stay for lunch.'

'Of course,' she said. When he had gone, she snatched up the scraps of her bikini and dressed herself, aware of a kind of shamed sanity. But for the intervention of these unknown Hamiltons, she would have a great deal to regret at this moment. Nothing had changed after all. She had known already that Blair could turn her to fire in his arms. But that had nothing to do with love. Only it would be easy, so easy to pretend that it did, she thought miserably as she trailed up to the house.

She could hear the sound of voices and laughter coming from the living room, but she bypassed it, going straight up to her room, where she showered shiftly and changed into a floating loose-sleeved, low-necked dress in shades of pink and deep red, tying back her dark hair with a matching scarf.

As she entered the living room, she was aware of a searching look from Blair, and she smiled composedly as he introduced her to his friends. They were near his own age, well-dressed, sophisticated but essentially good-humoured, and Courtney found herself liking them almost against her will.

'You'll think we're incredibly nosey, pushing ourselves on you at a time like this,' Abby said gaily. 'But when the rumour started going round that Blair was back, and had brought a *wife* with him—well, we just had to check it out.'

'And of course, in addition we're terribly nosey,' her husband put in, grinning. 'You're a close-mouthed bastard, Blair. You didn't say a word when you were here a few months back about planning to get married.'

'I wasn't sure then exactly what my plans were,' said Blair. He poured some fruit juice from a tall jug clinking with ice cubes and gave a glass to Courtney. 'At least I knew in the long term that Courtney and I would be married, but even I had no idea it would all happen so quickly.' He sat down on the arm of the chair she was occupying, putting his hand on her shoulder. It was all she could do not to flinch away from him, but she forced herself to sit still, to smile, to act the part of the happy wife.

Lunch was a fairly uproarious affair, and in the course of it Courtney learned that Jeff was in the oil business, an executive with a company engaged in test drilling only a few miles offshore on the other side of the island.

'Not the scenic side, fortunately,' he said with a slight grimace.

'I'll say it's fortunate,' Abby shuddered. 'There's nothing aesthetic about an oil rig!'

'Aesthetics be damned,' Jeff snorted. 'I suppose if I was in the luxury hotel trade and went about dotting huge lumps of concrete all over the landscape, that would be all right.'

'I'd say there's a place for both.' Blair intervened easily in what was evidently an old argument. 'Fashions in tourism change, and an island which has to rely on that fashion for its basic economy can't feel particularly stable.'

'But oil runs out,' said Courtney.

'Eventually,' Jeff nodded. 'But it doesn't go out of fashion. And there's talk of other things too—valuable mineral deposits in the mountains in the interior, for example.'

'Is that why you came here? To look for minerals?' Courtney asked, looking at Blair.

He hesitated, and Jeff spoke for him. 'Hell, no! He came here to lead the life of the idle rich—as evidenced, of course, by his purchase of this palatial residence. Only he found he couldn't stand it, and that's when he started looking for minerals,' he added with a chuckle.

Courtney put the glass she was holding down on the table with immense care, because she was afraid she might drop it. This—this was Blair's house? It belonged to him? She could not believe it, yet that was the inference to be drawn from Jeff's laughing remark. And she, like a naïve fool, had believed that it was just any rented house. And he had let her believe it.

Blair was looking at her, smiling a little, one brow lifted questioningly, as if he was reading her thoughts. She smiled too, but her steady gaze, meeting his, was cold and inimical.

It explained so much that had struck her as odd but unimportant—his familiarity with its layout, and the general locale, the warmth of the welcome from the servants.

If she'd pressed him, if she'd asked, 'How do you know so much about it all? Why are they all so friendly?' would he have told her the truth? Something seemed to close at the back of her throat, and she pushed her unfinished plate away, saying mendaciously that she was never too hungry in the heat of the day.

When the interminable meal was over, Jeff and Blair excused themselves and went off to talk. Abby and Courtney found a shady corner of the garden and Lena brought them a tray of iced tea.

'This is very pleasant.' Abby leaned back on her lounger, closing her eyes slightly. 'In fact, the whole day has been pleasant. Meeting you has been a lovely surprise.'

'I think we've all been in the market for surprises,' Courtney muttered.

'Mm?' Abby was not really listening, still pursuing her own train of thought as she looked up into the interlacing of branches and leaves above her head. 'I admit just for a moment there when we heard Blair was married, we wondered ... That is ...' she paused abruptly, as if realising too late what she was going to say might be construed as tactless.

'You wondered if I might be a blonde lady called Kate?' Courtney asked coolly.

'Well—yes,' Abby nodded rather guiltily. 'You know her, then?'

'Yes.' Courtney was silent for a moment, bitterness rising within her as she realised that Jeff and Abby must have met Kate here. That she'd been on the island with Blair, been at this house. She found herself praying inwardly, 'Oh, please—not in my room. Not in my bed.' She found her hands were clenched, white-knuckled, round the cane arms of her chair, and was thankful that Abby had not noticed.

'I didn't like her,' Abby said candidly. 'And neither did Jeff, for all he was knocked out by her looks. He thought she was a hard lady with an eye to the main chance. But she seemed—well established.' She looked at Courtney, smiling. 'We wouldn't have worried so much if we'd known of your existence. Obviously we got the wrong idea about her relationship with Blair altogether.'

Courtney moved her lips in a meaningless smile, at the same time fighting an impulse to pour the whole sorry story into Abby's ears. But she knew it was impossible. Abby and Jeff were Blair's friends, and any ill-judged confidences would only create an awkward atmosphere. No, it was better to carry on with her role of loving and beloved bride, and leave them their illusions, no matter what it cost.

'So where are you going after the honeymoon?' Abby asked, after a pause. 'Back to England? Have you a flat there? I remember Blair mentioning once . . .'

'I think he had a flat—but we have a house,' said Courtney. 'It—it's my old family home, actually. We lost it a few years ago—and when it came on the market, Blair bought it.'

Abby lifted her hands in the air. 'That's love all right. After all, he paid a small fortune for this place. Still——' she shrugged—'he can well afford it, placed as he is. Coming into all that money must have happened just at the psychological moment for Blair, because he's never looked back since. Money makes money, of course, and Blair has always been clever.'

Courtney's lips felt numb, but she made herself say, 'Yes.'

All Rob's hints, his bitter remarks came flooding back. So Blair had founded his new prosperity on stolen money after all. Nausea rose within her, and she fought an unpleasant little battle for self-control. She wondered how he had done it—how he and his uncle had managed to cover their tracks. She knew so little about these things, but she supposed that somewhere there had been a numbered bank account in a foreign country which specialised in such matters and asked few awkward questions. Thief, a little voice wailed in her brain, hypocrite, liar!

'Are you all right?' Abby was looking at her and frowning. 'You've gone very pale.'

Courtney sat up, swinging her legs to the ground. 'I think I may have had too much sun.'

'You'd better lie down for a while and draw the shades,' Abby directed kindly. 'Shall I come with you—or better still, shall I drag Blair away from Jeff?'

'Oh no.' Courtney sensed her rejection had been rather too vehement and sought to soften it. 'I—I mean, they're clearly talking about something important, and this——' she lifted a hand tentatively to her temples—'is rather my own fault.'

'Nonsense,' Abby said robustly. 'And Jeff and I

should be leaving soon anyway. But you and Blair must come over to us now that we've all met. We'll introduce you to the whole crowd at one of our beach barbecues. Some of them at the Club were only asking the other night when the next one was going to be, and now I have the perfect motivation.'

She insisted on taking Courtney's arm and leading her into the house, and in the cool hallway they met Lena, clucking anxiously, who took charge.

It was remarkably soothing to be put to bed in a discreetly darkened room as if she was a child again, Courtney thought, as she submitted helplessly to Lena's ministrations. It was nice to have a cool sheet tucked round her, and a cold wet cloth smelling pleasantly of some cologne placed across her forehead.

And while all these things were being done, while she had to smile and say thanks and acknowledge each service as it was performed, it stopped her thinking, and that was pleasant too.

But when Lena went out, treading softly and closing the door with exaggerated care, there was nothing left to keep the nightmares at bay.

The possibility had always been there in her mind, Courtney supposed, like a small festering wound. Once it had been suggested, it was impossible to disregard. Yet she had always hoped somehow that Blair's belief in his uncle's innocence was quite genuine, and not merely a cynical whitewash job to cover not only Geoffrey Devereux's tracks, but also his own . . .

And what could she do? Very little. Wasn't there some rule which forbade wives and husbands to give evidence against each other? And even Rob could do nothing without proof, and something warned her that proof would be hard to find. And even if the money had been in the form of a legacy from his uncle, Blair must have known where it had come from. Known, yet taken it anyway. Ruthless, Kate had said. Perhaps she too suspected the truth, but it wouldn't worry her. Anyone who saw a chance and took it would only rouse her admiration.

Perhaps Blair had only married her as some sort of extra insurance, Courtney thought wretchedly. But he was wrong if he thought marrying into the family would keep the Lincolns off his trail. Robin hated him. He wouldn't rest until justice was done.

The bedroom door opened quietly and Blair came in. He walked across to the bed and stood looking down at her and smiling.

He said lightly, 'Congratulations. That was very artistically done.'

'What do you mean?' Courtney's fingers caught the sheet and tried unobtrusively to tug it higher. She was suddenly agonisingly conscious that it was her sole covering.

He laughed. 'Getting rid of Jeff and Abby, of course. But you may have overdone it a little. I gather from various things Abby let fall as she was leaving that she suspects there may have been a more cogent reason than mere true love for our hasty wedding.'

Courtney's burning blush seemed to start from her toes. 'Oh, heavens! But that's impossible.'

'As I know only too well,' he returned drily. 'Is that what you wanted me to tell Abby?'

'No, of course not!'

'Then don't worry,' he said in some amusement. 'It wouldn't be such a big deal even if it were true. And it could easily have been—but for your brother's untimely interruption.'

Courtney turned her head away restlessly. She didn't want to be reminded of that.

She felt a movement and realised, alarmed, that Blair had sat down on the edge of the bed.

He said softly, 'But we shan't be interrupted this time, my lovely one. We're quite alone. Bertram and Lena have gone into town and taken Missie with them. Was that what you wanted?'

She said with a gasp, 'No—I wasn't making excuses. I—I have a headache.'

'I know a fantastic cure.' Blair took the hand that was clutching at the sheet and raised it gently to his lips, his mouth and tongue moving with unbelievable sensuousness against her palm. 'Darling, relax,' he whispered against her skin. 'I'm not going to hurt you.'

She was hurt already, wounded to the heart, confused and miserable. She hated herself for the way he could make her feel—for the way he was already beginning to make her feel in spite of everything. She hated her own heightened awareness of her body, the way she was conscious of every pulse, every tingling nerve-ending, the warm fluidity of the blood in her veins.

Blair leaned forward and kissed her very lightly, his tongue tracing delicately the outline of her mouth. Then he lifted himself away from her, and began to unfasten the buttons on his shirt, pulling it free of the pale cotton slacks which moulded his long legs.

He smiled down into her face, his eyes warm and slightly teasing.

'This time we'll start on equal terms,' he said, tossing the shirt aside.

Courtney said, 'No' in a strangled voice, and still clutching the sheet tried to roll across the bed away from him. There were no locks on any of the doors except the bathroom where there was a small bolt. It wasn't much, but it was all the defence she had.

But she hadn't reckoned on the hampering sheet. Blair moved fast, his body following her across the wide bed, his hands, imprisoning her, one each side of her squirming, terrified body.

'Let me go,' she said hoarsely.

'Like hell I will!' His voice was terse. 'Just what is this, Courtney? A belated attack of bridal nerves? I didn't notice much sign of them earlier, on the beach. So what are you trying to do—punish me for not telling you this was my house?'

'No!' she gasped. He was lying half across her, his weight bearing her down into the softness of the mattress, making her achingly conscious of her vulnerability. 'I don't care how many houses you have in whatever parts of the globe.'

'You've made that more than clear already—which is

why I decided not to tell you about Eden Rock, although I knew it was inevitable that you'd find out at some time. But you'd never ask, would you, Courtney? Because to ask about me—my possessions, my work, my hopes, my fears—might be the first chink in that barrier of aloofness of yours. But it's only a very fragile barrier, darling, because there's one sure way to break it down for ever.' His hand moved, stroking her bare shoulder, then slid warmly caressing down the length of her body, moulding the slender contours of breast, hip and thigh. 'And if you're wondering why I've held back all this time, my lovely wife, is because I was hoping, that the first move would come from you. But I'm not waiting any longer, Courtney. If this is all there is for us, then it will have to be enough.'

'Blair—no! She despised the pleading note in her voice. 'You promised . . .'

'And so did you,' he said flatly. 'In church, in front of witnesses. Not the plaintive little bargain you tried to make with me.' His hand took the sheet, peeling it away from her. 'Now I'm making the terms.' His fingers cupped and caressed, evoking a response it was impossible to deny. He said softly, 'And I'm warning you, Courtney, only your unconditional surrender will do.'

'You say I never ask you things,' she said huskily. 'I want to ask you something now, Blair.'

'Make it later,' he murmured against her burning skin, his fingertips pursuing a featherlight path over the flat planes of her abdomen. Her body felt as if it was melting with its need for him, but with her last vestiges of control she fought the insidious demands of his hands and mouth on her flesh.

'Now,' she insisted, and her fingers tangled in his hair, dragging at it, forcing him to lift his head and look at her.

'Well?' Impatience masked raw desire in his tone.

She took a deep breath, trying to steady herself. 'You have this house—you've bought Hunters Court. You may have property elsewhere—I don't know. But what I must know is—how did you do it, Blair?' Staring up into his face, she saw it harden, saw the warmth fade from his eyes, to be replaced by harsh contempt.

She was frightened, but she had to go on. She said, 'Where did you get the money?'

His mouth twisted unpleasantly. He lifted himself away from her and swung his legs to the floor, then he reached behind him for his shirt and shrugged it on.

He stood up, taking the edge of the crumpled sheet and pulling it up over her body.

Courtney propped herself up on her elbow, her wide eyes full of appeal as she stared up at him. 'Aren't you going to answer me?'

'I thought you'd already worked out the answer,' he said, coldly mocking. 'But if you really want it from my own lips, darling, then I'll gratify your curiosity. Let's just say that I—received it from a relative. And I hope knowing that makes you happy.'

As the door slammed behind him, Courtney turned on to her stomach, burying her face almost convulsively in the softness of the pillow.

So now she knew, and far from being happy, she knew that she had never been so miserable in her life.

CHAPTER NINE

IT was raining when they arrived back in London, one of those cold bleak grey days which totally belies the existence of an English spring, and it matched Courtney's mood exactly.

She had wondered more than once why they had not returned earlier. Why Blair had insisted on continuing with a honeymoon which was little more than a farce. As it was, following that night when she had forced him to tell her the truth, communication between them had dropped even below its former minimal level. They had been cold strangers sharing a roof, and there was no longer even a pretence at normality.

Bertram and Lena naturally asked no questions, but their bewilderment and disappointment was obvious, and the cheerful welcoming atmosphere in the house had undergone a steady insidious change.

Seeing other people had helped a little. Abby had been as good as her word, and in ordinary circumstances Courtney would have had the time of her life at the beach barbecue she organised in their honour. Other invitations followed, but if Courtney had assumed that Blair would refuse them, things being as they were between them, then she was wrong. Each and every one was accepted. They were out most evenings, usually not returning to Eden Rock until the small hours.

It was, Courtney thought painfully, possibly a more effective way of keeping her at a distance than sitting in hostile silence in the same room.

Yet she had no one but herself to blame. Hadn't she wanted to be at a distance? Hadn't she seen that as her salvation? She could hardly complain if she had been wholly successful.

She had expected they would spend the night in London, but that was not Blair's plan, it seemed. A car and a driver was waiting at the airport to drive her straight down to Hunters Court. Blair was remaining in London, alone.

Although he wouldn't be alone. That simply wasn't feasible. Courtney didn't think he'd found consolation for his frustration on the island, but he wouldn't be so reticent here in London where a willing lady awaited him. She could only be thankful that Kate hadn't actually come to meet them.

He spoke to the driver, giving him instructions, then came across to Courtney.

He said curtly, 'I'll be down at the weekend. By that time your father should have arrived and be settled in.'

She said almost inaudibly, 'I suppose so,' and made to turn away.

Blair put a hand on her arm, pulling her towards him, and his lips brushed her cheek swiftly and coldly.

Courtney stood and watched him walk away, and her hand went up to touch her cheek. Then, with a sigh, she got into the car.

The house was looking beautiful. The decorators had been working almost non-stop, and there was really very little left to do, Courtney thought as Mrs Garvin escorted her round.

There was a log fire in the drawing room, and tea with featherlight scones and a fruit cake laid on a low table in front of it.

'And the nursing home has telephoned, madam,' Mrs Garvin said as she handed Courtney her cup. 'Mr Lincoln will be arriving here tomorrow morning, with an accompanying nurse. Both rooms are fully prepared, but if you'd like to see them...?' Her voice rose questioningly.

Courtney shook her head with a faint smile. 'I'm sure everything's fine, Mrs Garvin. I'm rather tired after the flight. I think I'll have an early night. Perhaps—a light supper in my room?'

'Of course, madam.' Mrs Garvin, smiling approvingly, withdrew.

The supper was delicious, and the huge bed amazingly comfortable. But Courtney could not sleep. Hour after hour she lay awake, staring into the darkness, torturing herself with images of Blair and Kate together. She could imagine Kate's gloating triumph at her victory.

She tossed restlessly, deliberately blotting both of them out in her mind, but other problems swam to the surface in their place.

What was she going to tell her father? Blair's words had been, after all, tantamount to a confession of guilt. Did she have the right to withhold that sort of information from James Lincoln, who'd been so deeply injured by the Devereux machinations? She had little idea of the legalities involved, but the thought of possible police involvement—another scandal—made her feel sick. Nor would her father want that, she was sure.

Perhaps the purchase of Hunters Court and James Lincoln's reinstatement there had been some twisted form of reparation on Blair's part, although he hadn't admitted as much.

Brokenly she whispered, 'I wish I didn't love him. I wish I could learn to hate him.'

But even as the words were uttered, she already knew that was one wish that would never be granted.

She was firmly in control and smiling the following day when the ambulance arrived. She watched as her father was helped solicitously out and put in his wheelchair, then the chair was carried up the steps. Nurse Layton was young and plump and jolly, and she waved aside Courtney's rather hesitant explanations about why her patient's room was on the first floor instead of more conveniently on the ground floor.

'He doesn't spend all his time in his chair any more,' she said. 'He's doing very well with his frame. Besides, these stairs are broad and shallow, and I understand he's quite accustomed to them. We'll soon have him running up and down them,' she added breezily and, Courtney felt, over-optimistically.

To her untutored eyes, James Lincoln did not seem as well as he had done when she had seen him last a month ago. He seemed to have lost weight and his face looked strained again. He praised the arrangements in his room and bathroom, and told Courtney that the house was looking wonderful.

'And you—darling—happy?' He took her hand and squeezed it, searching her face with loving, anxious eyes.

She nodded, forcing gaiety into her smile, and began a small babble of words, telling him about the island, the beach, the parties, the barbecue.

'And the—hotel?'

She shook her head. 'It wasn't a hotel. It was a villa by the beach, called Eden Rock—very beautiful.' Now was the moment, if ever, she thought. She could tell him the house belonged to Blair and that would naturally lead on to everything else she'd learned. But the words wouldn't come. Something she was unable to explain kept her silent. Perhaps because her father looked ill again, and she was anxious to avoid any topic which could upset him.

They had dinner in his room, but he announced his intention of coming downstairs the next day.

'I want to see the house—see what's been done to it,' he said. 'Look at the gardens.'

Mrs Garvin brought in a tray of coffee. When she had departed, Courtney said, choosing her words carefully, 'How's Robin?'

Her father's face looked fretful. 'Well—enough. I think he regrets—deeply regrets—this estrangement.'

Courtney sighed as she poured the coffee. 'It was none of my choosing.'

'Perhaps not—but if you could—make the first move . . .' He let the words tail off hopefully.

'No,' Courtney shook her head, 'I don't think I could.'

He looked disappointed. 'Already Blair's come—between you—and your family. Rob was afraid—of that.'

'No, that's not true,' she said rather flatly. 'Rob behaved very badly. Whether he felt justified has nothing to do with it.'

'But if he came—here?'

'I wouldn't turn him away, naturally.' Courtney shrugged. 'But I don't think he'll come.'

'Ah.' James Lincoln looked reflective. 'Well—one never knows. It would be—nice. The three of us here again—like old times.'

She glanced at him under her lashes, masking her concern. How could he say such a thing? Couldn't he see that nothing could ever be again as it once was?

She said with difficulty, 'Daddy, this is Blair's house. He's not here at the moment, because he has a lot of work to catch up on—but he'll be here at the weekend, and we can't pretend differently. He's the master here now.'

James Lincoln winced, closing his eyes, and Courtney knew a pang of compunction as she looked at him. But it was no use leaving him with his illusions.

She was not altogether sorry when Nurse Layton came to interrupt them.

Her father seemed much more cheerful the next day. He walked round his room, using his frame, and in the afternoon negotiated the corridor outside his room, but Nurse Layton tactfully dissuaded him from attempting the stairs.

In the evening, Blair rang. Courtney despised herself for the lift of her heart when she heard his voice.

She didn't know what she'd been hoping for, but there was nothing in their brief exchange to give her particular pleasure.

'Is everything all right?' he asked, and then, oddly, 'No accidents of any kind?'

'None,' she said, puzzled. 'What were you expecting?'

'It doesn't matter,' he said dismissively.

'And what about you?' she asked crisply. 'Any problems at that end?'

'None that I can't handle.' He sounded faintly amused. 'I may be down before the weekend.'

A brief goodbye, and he was gone. As she replaced her receiver more slowly, Courtney thought that he might as well have spoken to Mrs Garvin.

It was while she was dressing the next morning that she heard the crash. She dropped her hairbrush and ran out on to the landing.

Nurse Layton was ahead of her at the top of the stairs, muttering vexedly to herself. She turned as Courtney came up to her and said crossly, 'I was afraid of this. I did warn him.'

Courtney put her hands to her mouth as she saw her father lying about halfway down the stairs. A walking stick lay nearby.

As they reached him, he lifted his head. There was moisture in his eyes, as he said, 'Not much good. Can't even manage—own bloody stairs.'

Between them and with some difficulty they got him back on his feet, and with Mrs Garvin's assistance, back to his room. Courtney waited outside anxiously while the nurse made a swift examination.

'He's not hurt, but he's shaken,' Nurse Layton said in a low voice, as she came out of the room and closed the door behind her. 'I'll call the doctor, I think, just to be on the safe side.'

'Yes, of course,' Courtney said mechanically. 'What made him do such a thing?'

Nurse Layton shrugged. 'He's made good progress, what with the therapy and everything. He wants to do more. I warned him at the start about too much adventuring.' She gave Courtney an odd glance. 'It isn't the first time he's had a go at those stairs. He seems obsessed by them, but I've always got him back safely before. I'd left him eating his breakfast, so he knew I wouldn't be checking on him for a while.' She pursed her lips. 'My goodness, I won't be taken in like that again!'

'It's my fault,' Courtney said distractedly. 'I should have insisted on a ground floor room.'

'Don't blame yourself.' The nurse gave her a consoling pat on the arm before she turned away. 'If you'd done that, he'd probably have been trying to climb the stairs instead.'

Courtney made herself eat some breakfast, but the image of her father lying crumpled and helpless robbed her of her appetite. She was thankful the stairs were so shallow. If they'd been steep and straight—she shuddered. It could have been a really terrible accident.

She sat up straighter in her chair, pushing a strand of hair back with an absent hand. What had Blair said? He'd asked if there'd been any accidents. And she'd asked what he'd been expecting . . .

Oh no, she thought, her hands clenching convulsively. Was that what he wanted to hear? That her father had fallen and broken his neck? That was hideous—disgusting in its implications.

While Mrs Garvin was clearing the remains of the meal away, Courtney went into the study. The furniture was different—a moss green carpet covered the floor, wall to wall, and the desk which stood in front of the large windows was a bigger, more workmanlike piece than its predecessor. But the panelled walls provided an atmosphere of cosy familiarity. This was one of the oldest parts of the house, and it had been left relatively untouched by the dictates of modernisation. Once, all the ground floor rooms had been panelled in the same elaborate way, but in the drawing room and morning room earlier generations had ripped it out to make way for the fashion of the day. Only the hall, the dining room and the study were still preserved in their original state.

Her father had always been particularly fond of this room. Courtney could remember long hours in the evening, curled up in a large wing chair beside the fire while he worked at his desk. He had mentioned the study wistfully more than once, and Courtney's heart had bled. With its French doors opening on to the terrace, and all the memories enshrined in its walls, this would have been the perfect room for her father, and yet her tentative suggestion had been dismissed out of hand by Blair, who had coolly informed her that he intended appropriating it himself. No concessions, she thought angrily. James Lincoln would live in his house on his terms.

She dialled the number of his London office, and was put through at once, after a brief but excited word of congratulation from the telephonist. As she waited, Courtney wondered whether this was the same girl who had talked so indiscreetly to Rob, and if she should have given her some type of warning.

Then she heard Blair say, 'Hello,' and all other issues faded.

She said thickly, 'I thought you'd want to be the first to know—we've had our accident.'

'What's happened?' he said sharply. 'Are you all right . . .'

'Don't bother to pretend,' she said scornfully. 'You know it isn't me. I didn't realise just how vengeful you could be, Blair! It wasn't enough to humiliate my father by making him live under your roof—you wanted the whole bit—an eye for an eye. Only it hasn't quite worked out. He's still alive.'

'Are you saying in your own inimitable way, Courtney, that your father's had a fall?'

'Yes,' she said. 'He fell on the stairs earlier. The doctor's coming, but it seems he's only shocked.'

There was a pause, then he said, 'I'm sorry to hear it, from a number of viewpoints.'

'Don't be such a hypocrite,' she said wildly. 'You knew all along he wouldn't want to be imprisoned in an upstairs room. Uncle Geoffrey died, and you won't be satisfied until my father's dead too.'

She closed her eyes, gripping the edge of the desk with her fingers as she waited for his reply.

Time stretched her nerves to screaming point as she waited—for what—an explosion of rage?

At last, unable to bear it any longer, she said almost pleadingly, 'Blair?'

'Yes, I'm here.' Not even the blurring of a long distance line could mask the ice in his voice. 'If you believe that, Courtney, then there's nothing more to be said. Goodbye.'

She heard the *clunk* as the line was disconnected, and for a long time she stood stiffly, clutching her own receiver, cradling it against her cheek as if by sheer willpower she could summon him back across the indifferent air waves.

Because the finality of that goodbye had terrified her.

She was summoned back to reality by the arrival of the doctor, who allayed her fears.

'He's trying to run before he can walk, my dear,' he said, as Courtney accompanied him back to the car. 'He needs to be patient with himself, as I've told him often. He managed quite well in the nursing home. Most of the time, he was a model patient. I'd have thought coming back to his old home would have had a calming influence. Can you think of any reason why he should want to be up and running?'

'No.' Courtney hesitated. 'Unless—he isn't on very good terms with my—my husband, as you must know, and perhaps he doesn't want Blair to see him in a chair or using a frame. It could be a matter of pride.'

'Courtney child,' Dr Reynolds said gently, 'a man in your father's condition can't afford that sort of pride. Slow and steady progress is what's needed, not leaps and bounds, or there could be the most serious consequences. I've put fear in him, or I hope I have. He's to rest in his room for the next few days and the nurse will keep him right with therapy.' He hesitated. 'Those stairs shouldn't present any problem— eventually—but you could consider providing one of those stair-lifts for the time being, if his inability to be at ground level is making him fret.'

'I'll mention it to my husband,' she said, and her hand stole to her mouth as he drove away, and she realised bleakly that she might no longer be in a position to mention anything to Blair again. Perhaps any future communication between them would be conducted through their lawyers, and that was a chilling prospect.

She walked for a while in the garden, trying to derive

some comfort from the burgeoning green spikes and buds, but neither the house nor the land could give her the peace she craved.

She thought in quiet desperation, 'I want Blair.'

As they set off on their honeymoon, he'd said, 'Alone at last,' but it hadn't been true, because too many ghosts from the past, too many fears for the future had gone with them. They could never shake off everything that had happened, and it would poison everything.

At Eden Rock that day, it had been so easy to let it all slip away, to be a woman with her man. If she had given herself, if they had belonged to each other in all the ways there were, at least she would have that to cherish. As it was, Jeff and Abby, with the utmost goodwill, had shattered her fool's paradise before it had begun.

To sup with the devil might hold an element of excitement, Courtney thought, her soft lips twisting bitterly. It was only later that you discovered how empty hell could be.

James Lincoln slept until lunchtime, and during the afternoon. Courtney had dinner with him in his room, and afterwards played chess with him. It was a game he enjoyed usually, but he seemed distrait and unable to concentrate, and when she began to beat him, he started to get irritable.

Putting the chessmen away, she'd asked him, trying to placate him, if there was anything she could get him.

He didn't look at her. 'Want Robin,' he said with something of an effort. 'Get Robin—here.'

She concealed her dismay, reflecting that their previous conversation on the subject seemed to have been totally overlooked.

She tried to smile. 'Of course, Daddy, if that's what you want—but are you sure he'll come?' she added carefully.

'Yes,' he said. 'He'll—come.'

When Nurse Layton appeared to make him ready for the night, Courtney went downstairs and telephoned the London flat. Rob wasn't there, so she spoke to one of his flatmates, briefly outlining the facts that her father had had a fall, and although there was no emergency, it was felt desirable to humour his wishes where possible.

'I'll tell him if I can catch him,' Lance promised with a laugh. 'He's leading a high old life these days, is Rob, although perhaps I shouldn't say so to his devoted younger sister.'

Courtney made some dutiful response in kind, thanked him and rang off. Only a matter of weeks ago, Lance's casual reference to the 'high old life' would have had her buzzing with concern. Now she could only feel indifference. At least under the circumstances, Rob wouldn't be calling on her good offices to get him out of any more tight spots, she told herself.

She wandered into the drawing room and sat down on the rug, looking into the fire, and let her mind drift, imagining how it might have been if the past three years had not intervened.

She thought of herself, waiting with passionate eagerness for Blair's visits. She imagined them wandering in the grounds together, talking about anything and everything. He would take her out in his car—to Hylam Abbey, perhaps, or to dinner. She imagined the growing happiness, the certainty and the burning need, and then Blair, asking her to marry him.

She shivered putting out a hand to the blaze. The dream began to falter there. Where would they live in all this might-have-been? Not here, certainly. At Eden Rock?

Her little sigh-held yearning. They could have been so happy there. She'd loved the house, and the island. Life could have been so good. But Eden Rock only existed because of the money Geoffrey Devereux had stolen. Any happiness she might have enjoyed there would have been stolen too.

Courtney buried her face in her hands. She wanted to leave this house. She wanted to drive through the night to wherever Blair was. She wanted to go on her knees to him, and beg him to return everything his uncle had stolen, so that they could get rid for ever of this load of mischief which was burdening them. She wanted to say to him, 'I love you. Let's start again from that moment in the rose garden when you kissed me. Let's find somewhere where we can live together, and learn about each other. It doesn't matter if we don't have any money. We'll manage like other people do.'

A little mirthless smile curved her trembling lips. She could manage, certainly. But Blair was frankly used to being a wealthy man. He wouldn't consider his luxurious world well lost for a dubious commodity like love.

He didn't need love, she thought painfully. She was just a pawn for him to use in his weird and complicated battle with her family. And if he needed sexual diversion there was Kate. Kate wouldn't want him to give up one iota of anything he possessed, whatever its legality or morality. The visible signs of success mattered to Kate, but not, Courtney thought, the means of acquisition. Another woman's husband, for instance, would be fair game . . .

She groaned, knowing what Kate must be thinking—what Kate would have guessed when Blair arrived back so abruptly in her life. Even she must have resigned herself to a period in the wilderness now that her lover had a new lady to initiate into the ways of passion, and it wouldn't take her long to discover the true state of affairs.

But what else could I have done? she asked herself miserably—and received no reply.

She drove into Wolverton the following day. Before her marriage, Blair had explained briefly and succinctly that he would be making her an allowance, and she needed to visit the bank to give them a specimen of her new signature among other details.

She had half wondered, as she sat in the manager's office, whether the arrangements that Blair had outlined would now be null and void, but she soon discovered that whatever their personal disagreements, the business

arrangements he had made on her behalf still stood. The
sum of money in deposit for her, to be transferred to
her current account when needed, made her gasp, and
there were credit cards waiting for her use, as well as a
charge account at the town's largest department store.

She had never had so much money in her life, or so
little desire to spend it. She wandered aimlessly round
the streets, but the only thing in any of the shop
windows she passed that caught her imagination was a
crystal sculpture of a single rose in a vase. A rose like
the one Blair had once given her . . .

It wasn't until she was inside the shop that she
realised it was the same jewellers where Blair had
bought her engagement ring, and the manager
recognised her instantly and came forward smiling to
serve her in person.

If he was disappointed that she only wanted to
make such a comparatively modest purchase, he
concealed it well, and the little rose was boxed and
wrapped with as much reverence as if it had been the
Hope diamond. Courtney tucked it into her bag,
wondering wistfully if it was an impulse she would
regret.

She drove home the long way round, going through
the village, and out of curiosity slowed outside the
cottage. It was occupied, she saw at once. There were
strange curtains at the windows and a large tabby cat
sat on the doorstep washing its face with a fastidious
paw. A small child came to the door, and seeing the car,
dashed back inside, presumably to tell its mother,
Courtney thought, letting up the clutch rapidly. She
didn't want the new tenant to find her staring in, or to
be involved in long complicated explanations.

Yet as she drove off, she couldn't help being glad that
it was a family now in occupation with children and pets.

'I'll get a dog,' she thought suddenly. 'It will be
company for me.'

And suddenly the irony of a bride of only a month
having to rely for companionship on a dumb animal
was too much for her, and she had to brake hastily,

bringing the car to a halt at the side of the lane.

Huddled behind the driving wheel, she cried as if her heart would break, thankful for the protection of the misted windows. Traffic passed—a tractor, a lorry carrying agricultural machinery, a couple of vans, the rumble of their tyres on the damp road surface concealing for a brief while the deep gut-wrenching sobs she could not control.

At last, inevitably, a car stopped, and Courtney, shaking, heard an authoritative tap on the driver's window. Slowly and reluctantly, she wound down the window.

Clive FitzHugh said, 'I thought it was your car. I had no idea you were back.' He paused sharply, 'What is it, Courtney? Are you ill?'

'No—no.' She scrabbled in the glove compartment for a packet of tissues, mopping at her eyes and cheeks. 'Just having a fit of female hysterics. I'm sorry you had to see me looking such a sorry sight, Clive, but thanks for stopping.' She made her tone deliberately dismissive, but he stood his ground, looking stubborn.

'I know that women cry,' he said. 'I have two sisters, in case you'd forgotten. I don't pretend to know what this is all about, but you look like death and you're obviously in no fit state to drive. So move over, and I'll take you home.'

She stared at him. 'But what about your car?'

He shrugged impatiently. 'It can stay here—I'll pick it up later. For heaven's sake, Courtney, I may not be fit enough to take part in the London marathon, but I can manage the few miles between here and Hunters Court without falling in a heap!'

'I don't doubt that,' she said rather humbly. 'It—it's very good of you, Clive.' She squeezed over into the passenger seat, and watched him take his place beside her, adjusting the seat position and the mirror.

'Yes, it is,' he said briefly. It was still there in his voice—the hurt, the bewilderment, even though he was masking it well. 'I thought brides were supposed to look radiant—not like leaky radiators.'

She gave a choky giggle. 'I think you've been misinformed. Didn't anyone ever mention a "period of adjustment"? And people cry for happiness sometimes, you know.'

'If you say so.' Clive's voice was blunt. 'Hellfire, Courtney, I don't want to pry into your private life. I know I haven't the right any more—if I ever had—but you look as if you're at the end of your tether.'

As he started the car and put it into gear, Courtney put a hand lightly on the sleeve of his tweed jacket.

She said gently, 'Please, Clive, don't read more into this than actually exists. I have all kinds of worries at the moment. For one thing, my father had a bad fall yesterday—the very thing he needs to avoid at all costs.'

Clive was immediately sympathetic, recalling an elderly aunt who had given their family nightmares by refusing to acknowledge that she was almost crippled with arthritis and embarking on one hair-raising exploit after another.

Courtney was thankful for the light, almost inconsequential chatter which took them all the way to Hunters Court. An unobtrusive glance in the mirror on the sun visor reassured her that although she was pale, and her eyes reddened, the aftermath of that storm of tears lay lightly on her.

'Would you like some coffee?' she asked as the car stopped at the foot of the terrace steps. She felt obliged to make the offer when he had been so kind, but her heart sank a little as he accepted, not bothering to conceal his eagerness.

Mrs Garvin met them in the hall, and Courtney asked her to bring a tray of coffee to the drawing room.

'At once, Mrs Devereux.' Mrs Garvin turned away, and then swung back. 'Your brother rang while you were out.'

'Was there a message?'

Mrs Garvin shook her head. 'He spoke to Mr Lincoln. The nurse took one of the extensions to his room so that he could do so.'

'Oh?' Courtney digested this. 'How is my father?'

'Resting, I think, madam. Nurse Layton is sitting with him.'

Looking round the drawing room, Clive said, 'I was going to say it's nice to see you back in your own home, Courtney, but I must confess I would hardly have recognised it.'

'Don't you like it?'

'I couldn't dislike it,' he said frankly. 'It's all quite beautiful.' He looked at her, smiling rather shyly. 'The perfect setting for you, Courtney. What a fool I was, letting the grass grow under my feet like that!'

She flushed a little, but tried to keep her voice light.

'Isn't that rather an exaggeration?'

'I don't think so.' He gave a slight shrug. 'I felt I had all the time in the world. How could I have known?' He spread his hands in a resigned gesture.

Courtney was regretting her invitation to coffee. Clive, she felt, was viewing their relationship in retrospect through some kind of rose-coloured spectacles. She had always known she would never marry him. He was pleasant to go out with, but she'd never seen him as a future husband, and she was pretty sure that until Blair's intervention, Clive hadn't been wholly serious either.

She said gently, 'Clive, we were never star-crossed lovers.'

'We were never lovers at all,' he came back at her with a trace of sulkiness. 'You always managed to keep me at arm's length, and yet you rush into marriage with a man like Devereux. I don't understand you, Courtney.'

'Perhaps I don't altogether understand myself,' she said, smiling rather painfully. 'Can we change the subject, Clive? This isn't going to get us anywhere.'

'Well, by all accounts this hasty marriage of ours isn't going much further anyway,' he said. 'You've been married a month, and he's in London, and you're down here. Not exactly togetherness, is it?'

'Nevertheless it remains our own business,' she said

steadily, meeting his gaze.

He flushed slightly. 'It's natural for me to be concerned,' he began defensively.

She shook her head. 'I've never given you that right, Clive. We were friends, that's all—nothing more.'

'When I find you crying your eyes out in your car, I claim my own rights,' he said stubbornly. 'Why don't you admit it, Courtney? Whatever the reasons for this weird marriage of yours, it hasn't worked out. Well, we're not living in the Dark Ages. There is such a thing as divorce. We're both young, and we could still be happy.'

There was real feeling in his voice, and Courtney cast a longing glance at the door, almost willing Mrs Garvin to arrive with the coffee.

She said quickly and coldly, 'You're being quite ridiculous, Clive, and taking altogether too much for granted.'

'I don't think so.' He shook his head. 'Devereux isn't here, and he should be. There was talk, you know, all the time you were engaged, about his relationship with that blonde assistant of his. Don't tell me you're so besotted you don't even care!'

He came over aggressively to the sofa where she was sitting, and before she could protest he leaned down, taking her hand and pulling her up into his arms.

He said thickly, 'I wouldn't leave you crying on your own, Courtney,' and kissed her, his mouth exploring hers with more eagerness than finesse.

She tried to push him away, but his arms were enfolding her like a strait-jacket, and she had to endure the kiss, praying that her sheer lack of response would cause him to desist.

That, she thought, thankfully hearing approaching footsteps and the opening of the drawing room door, or the arrival of the coffee.

Clive let her go at once, and she stepped back from him, instinctively putting up a hand to smooth her dishevelled hair, and wondering in acute embarrassment what Mrs Garvin had seen, and what interpretation she would place on it.

Only it wasn't a justly outraged housekeeper with a tray of refreshments who was standing in the open doorway. It was Blair.

CHAPTER TEN

ANY hope that he might not have seen her in Clive's arms was immediately dispelled by the expression of total and bitter grimness of his face.

He didn't look at her, and when he spoke to Clive, his voice was icy but controlled.

'Will you leave of your own accord, or will you be thrown out?'

Clive began bravely enough, 'Now just a moment, Devereux——' but as Blair took a step towards him, his whole attitude underwent a rapid transformation.

He said in a would-be conciliatory tone, 'All right—all right, I'm going. But you've only yourself to blame. I found her in tears earlier. I only wanted to give her some comfort—as you weren't here to do so.'

Then, when Blair's face showed not the least sign of softening, he brushed swiftly past him and vanished, and a moment later came the sound of the front door closing.

Trying to subdue a sense of rising hysteria, Courtney said, 'I'd forgotten! He drove her in my car. His own's miles away.'

'Then he can think himself lucky he can still walk,' Blair said curtly. 'It didn't take long, did it, Courtney, for you to find a shoulder to cry on?'

She said, 'I don't understand . . .' then, 'Oh, you can't think . . .'

'I don't have to think,' he said harshly. 'I saw—you, my wife—letting that pathetic little swine slobber all over you! What horror stories of my cruelty have you been regaling him with?'

She said, 'He was telling the truth. He did—find me crying, and he didn't think I was fit to drive myself home. He was probably right in that—but the rest of it was his own idea entirely.'

176

Blair laughed unpleasantly. 'You expect me to believe that?'

'I don't care what you believe.' Courtney shook her head wearily. 'You can hardly have the gall to accuse me after—after your own behaviour.'

'Most of the accusations to date have been on your side, darling,' he said. 'And with damned little evidence to support them. What the hell were you crying about that gave young FitzHugh the notion he had the right to comfort you?'

She shrugged her shoulders. 'What does it matter?' She turned away.

His hand took her shoulder bruisingly, whipping her round to face him. His eyes were blazing, and the scar on his cheek was white and throbbing.

'It matters enough to have brought me all the way down from London,' he bit at her.

'And all the way from Kate,' she flung. 'My, what devotion!'

His mouth thinned. 'Leave Kate out of this.'

'That's rather an old-fashioned attitude, isn't it? Turning a blind eye, and all that? Why not have an open marriage, where we both do exactly as we want and we both know it?'

'I'll tell you why not,' Blair said too softly. 'Because even the thought of you with another guy wrenches my guts.'

'You hypocrite!' she breathed. 'You dog in the manger! Do you think I—relish the thought of you with Kate Lydyard?'

'Why do you keep throwing her up at me?' he demanded roughly. 'Courtney, what's past is past. Let it lie—all of it.'

'It's easy to say that. Do you deny you're paying the rent on her flat?'

'Yes,' he said instantly. 'Kate occupies—or did—a company flat, one we keep vacant for visiting personnel from the States. It was a temporary measure while she was looking round for somewhere permanent to live.'

Courtney laughed scornfully. 'With you, no doubt!'

'That may have been her intention. It wasn't mine.' His grip on her shoulders gentled, as if he was going to draw her to him, but when she stiffened in resistance, he paused. 'Courtney, I'd be a fool and a liar if I tried to tell you that for the past three years there'd been no one—that I'd waited for you alone. And for a while, Kate was more than a business colleague. It was at a time when I was at a pretty low ebb. I saw no way of ever getting back to you, and I—remembered Kate from the old days. She'd been less than subtle then, about what she wanted, and there seemed no good reason not to take what was on offer the second time around. It was a physical thing, and it didn't last. I let her see that I felt it had been a mistake, and she seemed to accept it.' He paused again. 'There's something else you should know. Kate handed in her resignation the day we were married, and cleared her desk before we got back from honeymoon. Apparently she's got a job in Paris.'

A little flare of disbelieving joy was beginning to burn deep within her, but she forced herself to quell it.

'Distance means nothing these days,' she said stonily.

Blair sighed. 'Really? I know this—it means altogether too bloody much when it's between us—like this.' Firmly, brooking no opposition, he pulled her into his arms. He said huskily, 'I love you, Courtney, and I want you. I've made such a mess of everything, darling, because I wanted to prove so many things to you—justify myself in so many ways—and I've failed. All I've done is create this gulf, and it shouldn't be there, Courtney, not between two people who want to belong together as much as we do.'

She said in a strangled voice, 'I don't . . .'

A strained smile touched the corners of his mouth. 'Don't lie to me, darling. Your lovely, eager little body betrays you every time. It's doing so now.' His hand appraised with lazy sensuality the swollen curve of her breast, and she gasped in her throat. He whispered, 'Don't fight me any more, Courtney. Let our world and its problems go hang until tomorrow. That lout was right about one thing—I should have been here with you. Well, I'm here now, and I want you so much, my sweet.'

He was going to kiss her, and terrified, she jerked her head back.

'No, Blair, I can't! Do you think I could—make love with a man who wants my father dead?'

'What nonsense is this?' His brows drew together harshly.

'You can't deny it,' she said shakily. 'It's revenge, isn't it? His death for Uncle Geoffrey's. You asked about the accident because you were expecting—you were hoping he was going to have one. You knew he would fall.'

He said with immense bitterness, 'Yes, I was expecting it, and I wasn't surprised it happened—but I didn't want it, Courtney. I prayed I might be wrong.'

'Words—words,' she said distractedly. 'There can never be any life for us, Blair, not in this atmosphere of hate and mistrust.'

'Do you think I don't know that?' He released her almost contemptuously. 'I was a damned fool even to try and handle it this way. But it's over now, Courtney. At the weekend we're leaving for the States together. There's someone there I want you to meet. And after that, we're going back to Eden Rock.'

'No,' she shook her head, 'I can't do that. For better or worse, my place is here with my father. You made him what he is, Blair. If you truly want to make amends, you'll let me stay.' She swallowed, avoiding his gaze. 'I—I did order some coffee, but it doesn't seem to have arrived.'

'Mrs Garvin was bringing it as I came in,' he said bleakly. 'I sent it away, because I wanted to surprise you. I certainly managed that.'

Courtney bit her lip unhappily. 'It's getting late, Blair. I need to change for dinner. Can't we talk about this later?'

He shrugged, turning away from her to walk across

the room and look out of the window. 'Perhaps.' His voice sounded remote.

On her way to her room, Courtney glanced in to see her father, but he was asleep—to Nurse Layton's relief, she told Courtney.

'He's been very excitable this afternoon—in a very strange mood. It's taken me all my time to calm him down again.'

Courtney stared at her dismayed. 'You don't think— is it possible he could have another stroke?'

Nurse Layton gave her bright professional smile. 'Well, that's what we all want to avoid, dear. Perhaps— no chess or backgammon this evening. We'll just let him have a light meal and rest quietly, shall we?'

In her room, Courtney chose a dress from the wardrobe almost at random and tossed it across the bed, adding a handful of filmy undies as well. Her muscles, particularly in her face and neck were aching with tension, and the thought of a warm bath had an irresistible appeal.

She ran the water into the tub, adding some of her favourite scented oil, and tried to relax, but it was impossible.

She kept seeing the intent look in Blair's eyes, remembering the note in his voice when he'd said he loved her. Could she believe him, or was it just a convenient story designed to subdue her under his power for ever, so that she could never betray what he had done?

She left the cooling water and dried herself rapidly, then slipped on her old dressing gown. Her trousseau contained numerous other more glamorous garments, but she still tended to cling to the shabby comfort of this one.

As she stepped into the bedroom, she saw Blair. He was wearing a dressing gown too, a short brown silk one, and nothing else as far as she could judge, and he was lying in the centre of the big bed, watching her. His whole pose was relaxed, but it was belied by the intensity in his face.

She said nervously, 'What are you doing here?'

He raised his eyebrows. 'This is our room. Where else should I be?'

Courtney said weakly, 'You know—we had an arrangement . . .'

He said mockingly, 'I'm glad to hear you use the past tense. That's where that particular arrangement belongs—in the past, along with a lot of other things.'

Courtney bit her lip, trying to control the sudden trembling sensation which assailed her.

She said rather desperately, 'We—we said we'd talk later.'

He smiled reflectively. ' "Words, words", as you said downstairs. And where have they got us? Nowhere. Endless hurting, endless misunderstanding. I'm so tired of it, Courtney, and I think you are too. We've got to find some kind of understanding, some kind of meeting place before it's too late.' He held out his hand. 'Come here, darling.'

She swallowed. 'Blair, I should never have married you.'

'You never have,' he said quietly. 'A ceremony, however beautiful, doesn't make a marriage.' He lifted himself off the bed, and came across to her walking light as a cat on bare feet.

The very ends of her hair were slightly damp, and he touched them almost curiously, letting the strands curl round his fingers. He wasn't touching her in any other way, and it wasn't enough. She knew that with heart-wrenching certainty—knew that she wanted to be so close that nothing could ever divide them again. She stood on tiptoe and kissed his cheek, her mouth moving gently and sweetly over the scar, and his arms came round her, pulling her against him, his warmth and strength enslaving her.

The robe parted easily under his questing hands and slid from her shoulders to lie in a crumpled heap around her feet.

He whispered against her lips, 'Now take mine off,' and guided her hands when sudden shyness made her reluctant.

He lifted her and put her on the bed, then lay down beside her, kissing her, his mouth fevered and urgent against her cool skin, his hands moving with leisured expertise creating the first flowering of a pleasure so intense she heard herself moan in her throat. There was no room for doubt or mistrust any more, just this exquisite spiralling of need. Her hands touched him in turn, answering caress with caress, all inhibitions fled, her body moving against his with the same driving restless yearning.

Blair said huskily, 'I love you.'

'And I love you,' she whispered. 'Nothing matters beside that.'

'Nothing.' His voice thickened. 'Courtney, I've starved for you.'

Her hunger was as great. Not even her body's first pained response to the thrust of his invasion could fragment her utter abandonment, her total willingness to be one with him. And even that momentary discomfort was forgotten as tenderly and controlledly he took her with him over the boundaries of sensation to a realm of infinite and passionate delight.

She cried out in the final seconds of pleasure, and there were tears on her face, tears which Blair kissed away.

A long time later, she exclaimed, horrified, 'Dinner!'

'You can think of food at a time like this?' Blair's voice was lazily teasing, his hand gently and adoringly stroking her breast.

'Mrs Garvin—what will she think?'

He grinned. 'What should she think? I told her that we wouldn't be having dinner tonight, and let her draw her own conclusions.' He pushed the dampened tangle of hair back from her face. 'Do you really care?'

Courtney began to laugh. 'No.'

'That's my girl!' He kissed her deeply, his mouth lingering on hers. 'As it happens, I told her to leave some champagne on ice, and some smoked salmon sandwiches in the dining room. Shall I fetch them?'

She stretched delicately, no longer shy of the blaze of

his eyes down her body. 'It sounds wonderful!'

It tasted wonderful too. They fed each other, drank out of the same glass, and laughed a lot.

'Our wedding breakfast,' said Blair, smiling at her. 'The real one.'

She looked at him through her lashes. 'And what's for dessert?'

His smile widened. 'You are.'

This time their coming together was without haste, a slow mutual building to a shattering climax, and Courtney heard herself say again, 'I love you,' just before she drifted to sleep in his arms.

When she woke, it was very dark in the room, and instinct told her that it would soon be dawn. She lay very still for a moment, wondering what had woken her. Not Blair's soft regular breathing, certainly, although it could simply be that she was not used to sleeping with a man.

And then, quite inconsequentially, she thought of the rose she had bought that day, still in her bag down in the drawing room. It was a symbol, she thought, of that other rose Blair had given her all those years ago, but this one would never fade and die, and she knew she wanted it to be there at their bedside when he opened his eyes in the morning.

Moving carefully so as not to disturb him, she slid out of bed and put on her robe, knotting its sash loosely. Walking silently on her bare feet, she went out of the bedroom, and along the gallery to the foot of the stairs. She had reached the foot and was turning towards the drawing room when she noticed the crack of light coming under the study door. Someone had left the light on.

Mrs Garvin, Courtney thought, you've slipped up for once.

She was already turning the handle when the realisation that it could be an intruder first occurred to her, and by that time it was too late, because the door was opening, and her presence was known.

The sudden rush of light almost dazzled her. She

blinked, staring dazedly at the once familiar room with
the unfamiliar dark hole gaping in the panelling. She
looked at the man standing beside it, and said
unsteadily, 'Robin?'

'Yes,' he said impatiently. 'Oh hell, Courtney, why
did you have to come downstairs?'

She said, 'What are you doing here? And what's
happening?' She looked at the gaping space in the
panelling. 'Is that the priests' hole Blair mentioned?'
Her voice rose in disbelief. 'Then it does exist!'

'Oh, it exists all right.' Robin's tone was grim. 'Go
back to bed, Courtney, like a good girl, and forget you
ever saw me. Pretend you've been dreaming.'

'You knew about it,' she said, trying to get her
thoughts into some coherent order. 'You pretended you
didn't . . .'

'It was no pretence,' he said. 'I'd never heard of it,
and then I checked with Dad. And he told me all about
it,' he added rather heavily. 'Now get out of here,
Courtney, please. Let me do what I have to do.'

She moved further into the room. 'And what is that
precisely? I have a right to know.'

From the doorway behind her, Blair said, 'Are you
going to tell her? Or shall I?'

The bravado seemed to vanish from Robin's face. He
looked crumpled suddenly, and somehow shrunken.

'Oh no,' he muttered, half to himself. 'Now look
what you've done!'

Blair's arm came round her, hard and strong, and she
leaned against him as she looked stonily at the
strongbox on the floor, at the bundles of papers beside
it.

She said on a sound between a sob and a sigh, 'Ah—
no! Rob, it isn't true. Please tell me it isn't true!'

He said sullenly, 'It's true, right enough. You were
never meant to know, except at first—before it all went
wrong. Dad was planning to go abroad, you see, and
naturally he'd have taken us with him. But Devereux
guessed something was wrong, and started asking
questions. If it had all come out, Dad would have gone

to prison. He had to stop him, and so he made it seem as if . . .'

'As if Uncle Geoffrey had stolen the money himself,' Courtney said softly. 'Oh, how could he?'

Robin looked mutinous. 'I told you—he was desperate. He moved anything that might incriminate him down here, and hid it in the priest's hole. He'd always used it as a safe anyway, ever since Grandfather showed it to him. He'd got the money safely out of the country by this time, so he told Uncle Geoffrey some story—accused one of the accountants—I don't know. The guy had gone to Zurich, and Dad suggested that Uncle Geoffrey follow him there—and bring him back to face the music.'

'But instead he had Uncle Geoffrey himself arrested on a trumped-up charge.' Courtney felt swift nausea rise within her.

'Oh, don't be so bloody martyred,' Robin said contemptuously. 'If you'd stayed in bed with your ardent bridegroom, you need never have known. Dad was horrified when he realised Blair knew the priest hole existed, because he knew that he'd be looking for it—searching for evidence. He thought he'd be able to clear it himself, but he couldn't, so when I telephoned he told me what to do. I still had my key from the old days, and I came straight down.'

'So that was how he fell—why he fell.' Courtney covered her mouth with her hands.

Blair said, 'I blame myself for that, darling, but an innocent man wouldn't have made the attempt. I knew your father was guilty, and that he'd made my uncle the scapegoat, and that the proof was here somewhere. I told myself all I had to do was be patient.'

She was trembling. She turned in his arms, staring up at him, oblivious of Robin. 'But why didn't Uncle Geoffrey tell the truth? Why didn't he accuse Dad and save himself?'

Blair's mouth twisted wryly. 'Because he was his friend—and he loved him. And in his heart, he didn't really believe that your father would go through with it.

I thought differently, however, and that's why I came here that night to confront him.'

'Yes.' She swallowed. 'I—I think you'd better call the police.'

Robin made a startled negative sound, and Blair looked at her smiling a little, shaking his head. He said gently, 'No, my darling.'

'But you've got the proof,' she said almost wildly. 'All you've always wanted. There it is.'

'All I've ever wanted is here in my arms,' he told her softly. 'Yes, I was obsessed with clearing Uncle Geoffrey's name—with proving to you conclusively that he had always been worthy of the affection you'd shown him. He loved you, Courtney. He always hoped that one day—you and I . . . Before he died, he begged me to look after you. He was anxious for you. He'd discovered too late how unprincipled your father could be, and he had little faith in Robin either. He didn't want you to be hurt—in fact he'd have hated me for making you suffer as I have. And that's why I'm not going to call the police now—or ever. It's over, Courtney. Let it rest in peace. I'm not going to ruin everything we have going for us with some useless act of vengeance.'

'How incredibly noble!' Robin's voice was shrill and defensive.

Blair's face was icy with contempt as he looked at him. 'Don't push your luck,' he warned, soft-voiced. 'It would give me immense satisfaction to break your bloody jaw. And now you can return that key, and get out of my house.'

'Courtney——' Rob turned to her appealingly, 'are you going to let him . . .'

'Yes, I am.' She looked at him steadily. 'A crime was committed and you were prepared to help cover it up. I can't bear to look at you—or think about what you've done.'

Robin gestured at the box and papers at his feet. 'What about this?'

Blair's lips curled. 'Take them to your father,' he said

coldly. 'He's expecting you, isn't he? And a disappointment might be bad for his health.'

As the door closed behind Robin, Courtney felt the energy draining from her limbs.

'Darling.' Blair felt her subsiding limply against him, and lifted her, carrying her to the chair behind the desk. He placed her in the chair and knelt beside her, chafing her hands in his.

He said gently, 'You really had no idea, had you?'

'None.' She shook her head, a little sob rising in her throat. 'Oh, Blair, it's so awful! I loved Dad—I trusted him—I thought he was so wonderful—so injured. I've been so unjust!'

'Stop blaming yourself,' he said crisply. 'Uncle Geoff wouldn't want that, and neither do I. Your father is a lovable man—a charming man, but weak. And Robin's very like him, always looking for the easy way out. No doubt when you'd found yourself living in Rio de Janeiro or wherever, he'd have had a totally convincing explanation, and you'd have gone on for ever in your fool's paradise. But then his luck turned, and he became ill. He had money he couldn't touch, and he had to watch helplessly while he lost everything. There's a terrible justice in that somehow.'

She said in a low voice, 'Do you hate him very much?'

He shrugged. 'I—did for a time, but not any more. How could I go on hating the man who gave you life?'

'I wish you'd told me the truth at once.'

'You wouldn't have believed me,' he said ruefully, his hazel eyes tender. 'I told myself I had to get the proof, and the only place it could be was that damned priest hole. Every time I was here, I searched for it, but it's too well hidden. I was sure that your father would either make a superhuman effort to get to it himself, or persuade someone else to do so.' He paused. 'For a while, I was terrified it might be you, because I knew what it would do to you. It wasn't until I heard you on the telephone that day accusing me of wanting him dead that I realised what I was doing to you instead. I loved you desperately, and yet I was deliberately destroying any chance we had of being happy by letting you go on believing the worst about me.' He laughed bitterly. 'I even misled you over the money for Eden Rock.'

Courtney flushed. 'I was ready to be—misled, if that's how you like to put it. I couldn't understand how you were suddenly so wealthy. It made no sense.'

'At first it didn't make a great deal to me,' he said wryly. 'You thought that Uncle Geoff was my only relative. Well, I did too. I knew my parents had died when I was quite small, and that he'd been entirely responsible for my upbringing. What I didn't know was that my mother had married against her father's wishes, and had been cut off from them. After Uncle Geoff died and there was all the publicity in the papers, I was completely shattered. I didn't know which way to turn, and then out of the blue I got this amazing phone call.' He paused. 'It was from my grandfather in Texas. Apparently he'd been keeping tabs on me for some time, and had decided for reasons of his own now was the psychological moment to come back into my life.' He gave a short laugh. 'He was possibly quite right. At any other time, I'd probably have told him to go to hell. As it was I went over to the States, and we started to get to know each other. My mother had had a younger brother, but he'd died some years before in a freak fire at one of the oil-fields, so Grandad was setting me up as the long-lost heir. But I wasn't ready to be taken over, as I made more than clear, and I think he appreciated that.'

'Did you tell him everything.'

'Yes.' Blair's mouth quivered into a smile. 'He said, "Go nail the bastard". So then I told him about you, and he admitted that made a difference. "Still nail him," he said. "But nicely." '

Courtney shook her head. 'Blair, I can't face Daddy. Right now I feel as if I never want to see him again.'

'You will,' said Blair. 'We'll go to Texas and let my grandfather make a fuss of you, and then we'll take off for Eden Rock and have a proper honeymoon. By the time we get back, everything will be at a distance. You'll feel much better about it. He's an elderly sick man, Courtney, and you haven't got it in you to cut him out of your life completely. In a way he did what he did for you. He was in financial difficulties, and this house was costing him too much. He wanted to salvage something to continue giving you the kind of life you'd always been accustomed to. And the same for himself, of course,' he added drily.

'Of course,' she echoed. 'Oh, Blair——' her little laugh was scared, 'he could have ruined everything for us.'

'But he didn't.' He grinned at her, getting to his feet and drawing her up out of the chair and into his arms. She went willingly, her arms sliding up around his neck, and her lips parting eagerly for his kiss.

At last he whispered, 'Not that it really matters, but how did you come to be downstairs at precisely the right moment?'

'I came down to fetch something. A gift for you . . .'

He said against her lips, 'Come back to bed. You can give it to me there.'

Courtney began to say, 'But I didn't mean . . .' but as his kiss deepened, making her achingly aware of the fierceness of their mutual need, she knew with total certainty that their love for each other was, ultimately, the only gift that mattered.

Harlequin® Plus

THE STORY OF FAITHFUL PENELOPE

In *Sup with the Devil* Courtney wonders sarcastically if Blair Devereux expected her to "sit like faithful Penelope" for three years waiting for his return. She is referring to the age-old love story of Odysseus (often referred to as Ulysses, the Roman version of the name) and Penelope that the great Greek epic poet Homer wrote almost 3,000 years ago.

Odysseus was the king of Ithaca, an island off the west coast of Greece, and Penelope was his beloved queen. Because he was also a great warrior, Odysseus had to sail away to fight the Trojan War. The siege of Troy lasted for ten years, and on his journey home, Odysseus and his men were lost at sea. (His adventures as he made his way home are detailed in Homer's *Odyssey.*)

Many noblemen began to court Penelope, and begged for her hand in marriage. To put them off, and hoping that Odysseus might yet return, Penelope used many excuses. The most famous was the funeral shroud or "web" she began to weave for her dying father-in-law. She told her suitors she would marry when the shroud was finished. Penelope wove by day, and at night she returned to her loom to unravel all she had done. For three years this stratagem worked, until she was finally betrayed by a disloyal servant.

By this time, her suitors numbered more than a hundred, and they were making themselves comfortable at the palace, eating and drinking Odysseus's wealth away. They pressured Penelope continuously to choose one of them and remarry. Just as she was reluctantly about to give in, Odysseus returned—after twenty years' absence—and drove the boorish suitors from his palace.

The expression "Penelope's web" is still used to refer to any labor that appears endless. And because of her faithfulness to her husband, Penelope is thought a model of virtue. But considering Blair Devereux's past behavior, no wonder Courtney wasn't waiting like faithful Penelope for his return!